A Scoop of
A Cookie's Creamery Mystery
by
Kathleen Suzette

CW00404809

Copyright © 2023 by Kathleen Suzette. All rights reserved. This book is a work of fiction. All names, characters, places and incidents are either products of the author's imagination, or used fictitiously. Any resemblance to actual events, locales or persons, living or dead, is entirely coincidental. All rights reserved. No part of this book may be reproduced or transmitted in any form or by any means, electronically or mechanical, without permission in writing from the author or publisher.

Sign up to receive my newsletter for updates on new releases and sales:

https://www.subscribepage.com/kathleen-suzette

Follow me on Facebook:

https://www.facebook.com/Kathleen-Suzette-Kate-Bell-authors-759206390932120

Chapter One

"Ask me to tell you a joke."

I looked up from my menu to look at Noah. We were having dinner at the Seashore Café, and I was still trying to decide on what I wanted to order.

I smiled. "Okay. Noah, will you please tell me a joke?"

"Why did the detective break up with his girlfriend?"

My eyes widened, and my heart sped up. I had only been dating Detective Noah Grayson since the beginning of the year. Was he ready to break up with me? So soon? Had I done something he just couldn't get past? And was he going to do it by telling me a joke, and before I even got to order my dinner? I stared at him.

He grinned. "Why did the detective break up with his girlfriend?" he repeated.

I shook my head slowly. "I don't know. Why did the detective break up with his girlfriend?"

"Because she kept stealing his heart."

My mouth dropped open.

"Get it? Stealing? A detective can't date someone who's always stealing."

I laughed. I couldn't help myself. The look on his face said that he thought he was being very clever. "You're nuts. You've been saving that joke for me, haven't you?"

He nodded, taking a sip of his iced tea. "You know I have. You should have seen the look on your face."

I laughed again. Since I had begun dating Noah, I was seeing an entirely different side of him, and I liked it. "It was kind of cruel. You don't tell a joke like that to someone you've only been dating for three months. You should be ashamed of yourself."

He shook his head and closed his menu. "I'm not ashamed of anything. I've got jokes, and I intend to tell them."

I shook my head. "I bet you do. What are you going to order?"

"Turf and surf."

I nodded, still looking the menu over. I hadn't planned on dating Noah. When I first met him, he seemed cold and aloof. A jerk, even. Not that I was going to tell him that. Or at least, not yet. But he had asked me out at Christmas and I had said yes, and it might have been the best thing I had ever said yes to. Or at least, I hoped it would turn out to be the best thing I had ever said yes to. It was early days in our relationship, but I was happy as could be. We went out regularly, and we were enjoying ourselves. And now we had jokes to go along with our dinner. What more could a girl ask for?

"I think I'm going to get the shrimp and chips." I closed the menu and set it on top of his. "How did your day go?"

He grinned. "It went great. I only had one meeting today, and I wasn't spit on by any criminals, so it was a good day."

"No spit? You did have a good day then. I think you've got me beat." I thought about it for a moment. "Well, I never have any meetings at work, but I did have a kid throw his ice cream cone at me when he didn't like what his mother ordered, and I had no less than four middle schoolers roll their eyes at me."

He nodded appreciatively. "Sounds like you had an exciting day. Did the kid hit you with the ice cream cone?"

I sighed. "Left arm. Chloe says I've got to work on my duck and cover skills. She may be right. But I'd rather be hit by ice cream than get spit on, so maybe it wasn't so bad."

He grinned. "I wouldn't want to deal with the middle schoolers though, and they like their ice cream. I bet you see a lot of them. They can be feisty."

I took a sip of my iced tea. "They sure can be. Makes me really look forward to the summer when we'll be inundated by them. I can hardly wait."

He laughed. "Won't that be fun? You'll have all kinds of ice cream thrown at you then."

I smiled, shaking my head, and the waitress came and took our orders, then headed to the kitchen with them.

"What do you want to do this weekend?" he asked. "I've got it off. We should do something."

Before I could say anything, he said. "How about deep sea fishing? Do you like to go deep sea fishing? Or surfing? How about surfing?"

I shook my head and sighed. "I have to work. I told Cookie I would work the afternoon shift." Now I was sad that I had volunteered, but it was spring, and with warmer weather, things were picking up at the ice cream shop. My best friend Chloe's mom owned the ice cream shop, and she was working on hiring back some of the employees she had to lay off during the winter. I was going to be glad to see them return to work.

"Oh, that's a bummer. Maybe the following weekend? We can just get something for dinner this weekend if you want."

"I'll try to get the next weekend off. But I've never been deep sea fishing, and I don't surf. And dinner would be great."

His brow furrowed. "Wait. You grew up in a small town on the California coast, and you've never been deep-sea fishing, and you don't surf? I don't know what to think about that."

I chuckled. "I get seasick, and my lack of balance on a surfboard is extraordinary. A thing to behold." It wasn't for a lack of trying with surfing. I just couldn't stay upright. And having that board strapped to my ankle made me a little claustrophobic. Maybe it was silly, but I kept imagining the board whipping around and hitting me in the head or that it would somehow move over on top of me and hold me beneath the water. Neither of these scenarios made sense since surfboards don't weigh much, but there you have it. The reasons I don't surf.

"I see. You're balance challenged."

I nodded. "That's one way of putting it. Maybe we could just go to the beach and hang out? It's one of my favorite things to do."

He nodded and took a sip of his iced tea. "That sounds like a plan. We could bring a picnic lunch."

"That sounds like fun." I smiled. Being with Noah made me feel almost giddy.

Chapter Two

When I got home from our date, I made myself some cocoa and sat on the couch to watch television for a few minutes. My orange tabby, Oliver, climbed in my lap and immediately went to sleep. I only intended to stay up for a few minutes, just until I finished my cocoa. But when I did finish it, I didn't want to wake Oliver, and I got interested in a true crime show. Before I knew it, it was almost midnight, and I had the opening shift at the ice cream shop.

I groaned. "Oliver, I'm going to feel miserable in the morning." He meowed when I set him on the couch and headed to bed.

I was asleep before I knew it, but I woke up at 4:15 and even though I was tired, I couldn't get back to sleep. I tossed and turned, thinking about work, Noah, and the things that needed to be done around the house, and sleep just wouldn't come. Oliver had followed me to bed last night and now he got tired of me bumping him as I moved around and he jumped to the floor, wandering into the living room to find someplace a bit more peaceful to sleep. I groaned.

At six o'clock I sat up, blinking in the dim light. Even if I could fall asleep, at this point, it was too late to do me much good, so I decided that I had better work on being fully awake instead. Giving up on the idea of getting more sleep was painful, but it had to be done. I got dressed and put some athletic shoes on. I was sure I would feel better if I took a short walk so I made a quick cup of coffee, pouring it into a travel mug, and grabbed my phone and keys.

The sun poked its head up over the mountains as I walked briskly along the street that would take me to the beach. Thankfully I didn't live far from it, so I could take a walk there to see what was going on. The cool air and the exercise made me feel a little better, and the coffee sure didn't hurt. A light breeze blew, and I brushed my hair out of my face.

When I got to the edge of the sand, I had to make a decision. Keep walking on the side of the road, or take my shoes off and walk on the sand? I hated the idea of taking my shoes off, but the beach was so peaceful and quiet that I really wanted to walk along the water's edge, so I decided to take them off. I tucked my socks inside my shoes, tied them together, and put them over my shoulder.

The sand was cool on my feet as I walked and pulled at my calves. I wished I was in a little better shape as my legs burned with the effort.

On my left was a huge rock the size of a small hill, but shaped more vertically than most hills. It had been a hangout for Chloe and me when we were in high school, and it always brought back happy memories. A narrow dirt walkway went around the rock and opened up on the other side. It would only take a few minutes to walk it. I glanced at my phone. I had the time.

As I got to the entrance to the path, I almost ran into a woman coming from the opposite direction. She was looking down as she walked, and her eyes widened when she looked up and saw me. "Oh!"

I smiled. She had the prettiest green eyes I had ever seen. She had a large beach bag over one shoulder and wore a sun visor. "Good morning. Out for a little walk?"

She smiled and nodded, her short black hair bobbing with the motion. "Yes, there's nothing like a nice long walk early in the morning. Have a nice day!"

She hurried past me and out onto the beach.

"You too!" I called. She must have been one of those speed walkers because she was really moving.

I walked onto the narrow path, sipping from my travel mug. The woman was right. There was nothing like taking an early morning walk when everything is peaceful and there's no one around to interfere with your thinking.

The one drawback to the path was that if you ran into someone, one of you had to squeeze over so the other could pass, or someone had to turn around. Passing wasn't impossible, but it was a real squeeze.

The breeze kicked up, blowing my own short black hair into my face. I tucked it back behind my ear and took another sip of my coffee. If I could manage to get to bed at a decent time at night, I could make this a habit. I glanced at the sun as it rose higher, glinting off the ocean. There was a metal railing that kept people from getting too close to the edge of the path and accidentally falling into the water, but when we were kids, we had jumped off the railing more than a few times. Ignoring the warning signs at either end of the trail probably wasn't the brightest thing to do, but we did it. And it brought back more great memories as I walked.

I got to the end of the path, then wandered along the side of the rock where a few scrub trees grew, and families of squirrels lived. If I had thought about it, I would have brought them some nuts to eat. I walked until I got to the alcove on the side of the rock. The road was only a few hundred feet from here and there was a picnic bench tucked back into the alcove. As I approached it, I noticed something on the ground. For a moment, I thought it was a dark beach blanket someone had left behind, but as I got closer, I realized it was a person. I turned aside, thinking it must be a homeless person. I didn't want to disturb them. Only, that didn't seem quite right. I stopped, staring at them, then decided to move a little closer.

I pulled my phone from my pocket and glanced at it to make sure I had service, then moved in a little closer. That was when I thought the form looked familiar. I hurried closer.

Mr. Franks.

Chapter Three

In a daze over finding Mr. Franks' body, I called Noah, and he promised to be right there as soon as he got dressed.

Mr. Franks was an elderly man, I guessed somewhere in his late seventies, who searched the local beaches with his metal detector almost daily. He was faithful to his work, carefully going over the areas with a fine-tooth comb, while getting an early start each morning. He was pleasant to talk to and he loved the daily hunt for treasures. His metal detector lay about ten feet from him and the canvas bag he always carried over his shoulder to bring home his found treasures was lying beside him, open. From where I stood, I could see something metal poking out of the mouth of the plain canvas bag, along with a handful of small shells. It was then that I remembered that Mr. Franks liked to collect seashells, as well as the treasures he found on the beach. For some reason, that made me sadder than I already was about finding him dead like this.

The cool breeze ruffled my hair, and I set my coffee cup down, giving the cup a turn in the sand to make sure it stayed upright, then wrapped my arms around myself, wishing I had brought a heavier jacket. While I was walking and working up a sweat, I hadn't noticed how chilly the air was, but now that I was standing still, I realized just how cool the early morning air was. I half-turned to look at the trail behind me, but it was empty. I sighed as seagulls dived into the ocean and called to one another above the rush of the waves, going on with their lives, unaware of what had happened just yards from them. I turned back to Mr. Franks, wishing I had something to cover him up with.

I swallowed and moved toward him, suddenly wondering if I was right in that he was dead. He was, wasn't he? I stepped closer. Mr. Franks' eyes stared lifelessly up into the sky, making me shiver. I look away. 'The poor thing,' I could hear my grandma Pearl say in my mind.

I swallowed and moved in closer, my eyes on the canvas bag. There was a small lump inside of it and I wondered what Mr. Franks had found this morning. The thought made me sad. He'd been out here doing what he loved to do and someone had killed him. Maybe they had thought he had found some real treasure, and they tried to steal it from him and he had resisted. Maybe if he had just handed the bag over, he would be alive with just a story to tell. They must have rushed off, leaving the bag behind when they realized they had killed him.

I sighed, glancing at his head. There was blood seeping into the sand. Shaking off what I had just seen, I moved in closer and squatted down, looking at the opening of the canvas. There were several different types of shells, a sand dollar, and a small ladies' ring that was corroded from the damp sea air. There had once been a small stone in the setting, but it was long gone. Why had he felt the need to pick it up and take it with him? It couldn't be worth anything. It was hard to even tell whether it was silver or gold, it was so corroded.

I scooted forward to get closer to the bag. There was a quarter, sticking out from beneath the edge of the bag. What was the lump further down in the bag? Did I dare to open it and see?

The sound of footsteps in the sand and someone's mildly labored breathing came to me, and I stood up, turning to see who was there. Noah came into view, walking around the side of the rock, and I let my breath out. He gave me a grim smile and a nod.

"Hey."

He nodded again and came to stand beside me. "Hey."

"It's Mr. Franks."

He glanced at the body. "I don't think I've had the pleasure of meeting him." He walked over to him and examined the blood coming from the back of his head without moving him. He glanced over at the metal detector. "Looks like whoever killed him had a strong swing. Unless it's a bullet wound, and the bullet didn't come out the other side."

"He came out here almost every morning to find treasures."

He glanced at the metal detector again, then straightened up and went to look at it. After a few moments, he looked back at me. "This might be our murder weapon. There's blood on it. I've got some backup on the way and a call into the coroner's office." He set down a little yellow triangle with the number one on it near the metal detector and took a picture.

I shook my head. "This makes me so sad. He would come into the ice cream shop sometimes and tell us what he'd found.

Sometimes, if he came right after he finished treasure hunting, he would show us stuff. It made him so happy to find these things." I suddenly felt like crying. Why would someone want to kill such a sweet man?

His brow furrowed as he glanced at Mr. Franks. "That's a real shame. Did he ever say he found anything of real value? Maybe someone tried to rob him."

I shook my head. "If he did, he didn't tell us. Sometimes he found some coins, sometimes some jewelry. One day he said he found a man's class ring from 1959, and he was so excited about it. He kind of made up this story about the owner being a high school kid back in 1959. He and his girlfriend went to the beach the day after they graduated high school, and he lost it, and it had been buried beneath the sand all this time. He had a vivid imagination, telling us stories about some of the things he found. I think it just gave him something to do in his retirement."

He nodded and went back to look at Mr. Franks. "Was he married?"

"I think he once said that his wife died years ago." The breeze kicked up again, and I shivered.

He took pictures of the canvas bag. "No one has moved these things, right?"

I shook my head. "Not while I've been here. What's that lump in the bag?"

He glanced at me. "Patience, Watson. I don't want to disturb anything until I get pictures of everything visible, then I'll take a look at the inside of the bag, his pockets, and anything else that needs looking into." He smiled. "What are you doing out here so early?"

I shrugged. "I couldn't sleep, so I decided to go for a walk."

He nodded as we heard sirens in the distance. "Well, I'm sorry you came across him like this."

"Me too."

Seeing Mr. Franks dead like that made me feel a little sick. Of all the people I knew in Lilac Bay, he was the last person I would have thought someone would have murdered. But if someone thought he was carrying treasure in that bag, then it was probably just a robbery that went badly.

Chapter Four

I stopped by the Whole Bean Coffee Shop and picked up vanilla lattes for Chloe, Cookie, and myself before going to work at the ice cream shop. A double shot of espresso was in order. I wasn't looking forward to going to work, because I was exhausted by the time I left Noah at the beach to investigate the murder. When I first spotted Mr. Franks, the adrenaline had coursed through my body, making me feel like I could run a marathon, but now that the adrenaline had dissipated, I felt like I had actually run one, and all I wanted to do was go home to bed.

I smiled as I entered the kitchen at Cookie's Creamery. "Good morning! Look what I brought." I held up the drink carrier.

Chloe smiled. "Oh, Maddie, you are a lifesaver." She hurried over to me and took one of the cups from the carrier. "How did you know that I needed coffee?"

I sighed and smiled. "I guess I'm a mind reader this morning." I handed a cup to Cookie.

Cookie's eyes widened. "Thank you, Maddie. That was sweet of you to think of us when you picked yours up." She took a sip. "Perfect. Just like I like it."

At Christmas we had begun selling plain jane coffee and cocoa to go along with the cookies to boost our business and it had helped immensely, but with the weather warming up, Cookie had decided to put the coffee maker and cocoa maker away until next year.

"How is the ice cream making coming?" I asked as I stowed my purse and grabbed a clean apron from the drawer. I sighed again, then chugged my latte. I needed that caffeine to kick in soon, or I was going to be asleep on my feet.

"It's going swell," Cookie said, looking up at me from the machine she was standing next to. "That's the second sigh. What's going on?"

I smiled in embarrassment. "Am I sighing? I can't seem to help myself this morning. I have bad news." I filled them in on what had happened at the beach.

"Oh, poor Mr. Franks," Chloe said. "I can't believe someone would do that to him."

Cookie shook her head. "What a shame. What's this world coming to?" She poured more heavy cream into the ice cream machine. "I suppose Noah is on the case?"

I nodded and looked at the whiteboard to see what needed to be made this morning. "Yes, I called him, and he came right away."

"Is Mr. Franks married?" Chloe asked as she went to the industrial-sized refrigerator and got some milk out.

"I seem to remember him saying his wife died about twenty years ago. I don't know about any other family he might have locally." I wished that I knew more about him. He had been a pleasant customer who loved to tell us stories about what he had found when he stopped in. I was going to miss him.

I LOOKED UP AS THE bell over the front door jingled, and Estelle Smith walked in. She was wearing a purple pullover sweater, Capri jeans, white canvas athletic shoes, and a big smile. That was Estelle. She loved to smile.

"Good morning, Estelle. How are you?"

She nodded and stepped up to the counter. "I'm the bees' knees this morning, Maddie. What have you got for me today?"

I leaned on the counter. "How does raspberry chocolate truffle ice cream sound? I've already tasted it, and Cookie outdid herself."

Her eyes widened. "It sounds delicious. How about a scoop of that in a waffle bowl and a drizzle of chocolate syrup?"

I nodded and got the bowl. "And for your free cookie?" At Cookie's, we gave away a free cookie with each ice cream purchase. The customers loved and we got lots of repeat business because of it.

She glanced over at the cookie display case. "How about a double fudge chip?"

"You got it." Chocolate was Estelle's favorite. In fact, you could say that it was per passion.

"I saw a bunch of police cars and the coroner's van down at the beach when I took my walk this morning. You wouldn't happen to know what's going on, do you? Someone said it was that fella who's always looking for treasure on the beach. You and I both know that's Leland Franks, but I can't imagine what could have happened to him." She looked at me questioningly.

I sighed for what had to be the fiftieth time this morning. "Don't tell anyone, but it *was* Mr. Franks. I found him when I was going for an early morning walk."

She made a zipping motion across her lips. "My lips are sealed. I won't tell a soul. It wasn't an accident, right? I have a feeling that it wasn't, based on how many police cars there were."

I shook my head. "I haven't heard back from Noah, but no, it wasn't." I knew Estelle would keep things quiet, but I did feel a little guilty about talking about it.

She shook her head. "What a shame. I went to school with him, you know."

"High school?"

She nodded. "Yes, high school. He married one of my friends, Margaret Adams. She wasn't a close friend, but she was still a friend."

Chloe came out of the kitchen carrying a tub of ice cream. "Morning, Estelle."

"Good morning, Chloe." She turned back to me. "He was real broken up when Margaret died."

Chloe set the tub of ice cream in the freezer and hurried over. "Mr. Franks?"

I nodded. "Did they have any kids?"

"I don't think so. But he has a live-in caretaker, so he wasn't completely alone. Lucy Jacobs. I think he had her more for the company than anything else. Leland wasn't infirm. He got plenty of exercise walking the beaches looking for treasure. Oh, and a nephew. He did have a nephew he was close to."

We looked up as a woman walked through the door. My brow furrowed as Chloe stepped up to help her. She looked familiar, but I wasn't sure why.

"Good morning. What can I help you with?" Chloe asked her.

She smiled, tucking a lock of her black hair behind her ear. "I'd love a scoop of rocky road on a plain cone."

"Good morning," I said to her as I scooped Estelle's ice cream. "It sure is pretty out this morning."

She smiled. She wore bright red lipstick that accentuated her pale complexion and a dark blue hoodie. "It certainly is. This is the life, isn't it? All the sun and water you could ever want." She chuckled. "I just moved to town from Wisconsin, and I'm not going to miss the snow one bit."

"I don't blame you," Chloe said. "I couldn't handle all that snow. I'm a beach girl."

"Lilac Bay is my favorite place in the whole world," Estelle said. "Welcome!"

The woman smiled again. "Thank you. I think I'm going to enjoy living here."

I drizzled some chocolate syrup on the ice cream I had just scooped and then got Estelle's cookie for her. Where had I seen this woman before?

Chapter Five

C hloe and I had the following day off, and we decided to take a walk on the beach. The weather had turned out warmer than expected, giving us a preview of what summer would hold. A light breeze brushed my skin, and I smiled. I was a summer girl all the way.

I bent down and took off my sandals, holding them in my hand as we walked onto the beach's loose sand. Though it was warm, only a few beachgoers were lying out in the sun. It was the middle of the week, so we wouldn't see many sunbathers until the weekend.

"I still can't get over the fact that Mr. Franks was killed."

I glanced at Maddie as she put one hand up to her forehead, scanning the horizon in the bright sunlight. I nodded. "I can't believe it either. I mean, I get that maybe somebody was trying to rob him, but kill him? He was just an elderly man enjoying his retirement, and now he's gone."

She nodded. "Let's go talk to Bill Washington at the bait shop."

I nodded. "I was thinking the same thing." Bill had owned the bait shop at the north pier for decades and was a friend of my father's. He sold drinks and snacks, along with bait and other fishing supplies.

When we got to the tiny bait shop, there was no one inside, other than Bill. He looked up from the newspaper he had spread out on the counter and smiled. "Well, good morning, ladies. What brings you out to my humble place of business?"

I smiled, and we headed up to the counter. "Good morning, Bill. We were out taking a stroll along the beach since the weather is so nice, and then we decided we needed to stop by and say hello. I'm also practically dying of thirst." I glanced over at the refrigerated cooler that held water, soft drinks, energy drinks, and pre-made sandwiches. If you were going to spend the day fishing, this was the place to stop and pick up just about anything you might need. There were even fishing poles on display in the corner of the shop in case you left yours at home and decided you wanted to go fishing once you got here.

"You came to the right place. Did you ladies hear the sorry news?

I turned to him. "About Mr. Franks?"

He nodded. "Yes, ma'am. Leland Franks. It sure is a shame that someone went and killed him like that."

"We're still in shock about it too," Chloe said. We moved over to the cooler and opened it up. I grabbed an orange soda, and Chloe grabbed a strawberry, just like we had always done when we were kids. We brought them back to the front counter.

"Did you know Mr. Franks well?" I asked Bill.

He nodded. "I guess I knew him about as well as I could. He stopped in nearly every morning, you know. Out there treasure hunting with his metal detector. He'd find some neat things now and then, and he'd always come by to show them to me. He also stopped in to get a soda or some peanuts to eat to keep his energy up." He winked. "Bill was devoted to his hobby."

I nodded. "He would stop in at the ice cream shop too, and sometimes he would show us what he found."

He grinned. "That sounds like Leland. Maddie, I heard you were dating that detective fella?" He said it as a question, but that bit of news had traveled quickly around town and I was sure he knew that I was.

I nodded, smiling. "Yes, Noah Grayson. He's working on the murder case. The truth is, I found Mr. Franks' body."

His eyes widened. "Oh, my goodness. That must have been an awful sight to see. I'm sorry that you had to see that."

I sighed. "I wish that I hadn't. Did Mr. Franks ever mention to you that he was having trouble with anyone?" Although I figured that he had probably been robbed, there was this thought at the back of my mind that said maybe that wasn't what happened.

He thought about it for a moment. "Well, he did have a nephew that bothered him from time to time. He was always asking to borrow money I guess, and it really bothered Mr. Franks. Eddie Franks. Leland said he was well past the age when he should be supporting himself, and I guess all he ever did was work part-time jobs, or jobs that didn't add up to much. Do you know him?"

"I do," Chloe said. "He worked for my mother a few years ago. It was only a part-time job through the summer, and you're right, it didn't seem like he had ever had a job that could have become a career or that would pay much."

"I don't know him myself," Bill said. "All I'm going by is what Leland said. He was adamant that his nephew wasn't worth a whole lot. But other than that, I can't think of anybody else he was having a problem with. But I really doubt that his nephew was much of a problem. It sounded like he was more of an annoyance." He chuckled. "Leland was something else. He was always so excited about the little things he found out in the sand. Occasionally, he found things that were worth a few dollars, and he would sell them at the pawnshop. But really, it was just something to do to take up his time."

"So he did find things that were of value then?" I asked. It was hard for me to believe that there could be much of anything valuable buried out there in the sand. But I might have been wrong.

He nodded. "Oh, sure. He found old coins occasionally, and jewelry. Sometimes the jewelry was in pretty rough shape, but he said Tom Robinson, the owner of the pawnshop, would give him a few dollars for it. It didn't matter if the jewelry was in bad condition as long as it was silver or gold because Tom would buy it and then sell it to somebody who would melt it down and make it into something else."

I nodded. "I guess that probably kept him going then. Just the thought that he might find something of value."

Bill nodded. "Oh yeah. It was exciting for him." He chuckled. "He found a nice wedding ring once. It was a ladies' and was gold and had a half-carat diamond in the setting. He sold it for a few hundred dollars, I think. I don't think he needed the money exactly; it was just fun for him when he found things like that."

"I bet it was," Chloe said. "I've always thought about doing that someday. Getting a metal detector and just hunting around for a day or two to see what I could find. But I think that the chances of finding something on your first day out are just about zero, so I've never been terribly motivated to try it."

Bill chuckled and rang up our sodas, and I grabbed a package of chips and sat it next to them. "I told Leland I was going to give it a shot once I retired. Trouble is, I don't know if I'm ever going to get a chance to retire. I don't know what I would do with myself if I didn't come here every day."

I nodded. "I think if you're going to retire, you're going to have to come up with a plan and figure out things to keep yourself occupied. Or at least, that's what I'm going to do."

He chuckled again as I paid for the chips and sodas. "That is an excellent idea, Maddie. I'm going to have to take it under consideration. But I don't think I'll be retiring this year."

"Good. We'd hate to not have you to visit with when we come to the beach."

He flashed me a smile. "Well, thank you, Maddie. I appreciate hearing that, and I appreciate seeing the two of you stop in now and then."

We talked to him for a few more minutes before leaving. I wondered what the trouble was between Mr. Franks and his nephew and whether it was really just an annoyance, as Bill said, or whether it was more than that.

Chapter Six

After we finished talking to Bill at the bait shop, we decided to take a drive down to the pawnshop. I hadn't been in there since I was a kid and I wondered if it had changed any. My memory said it was a dark, musty shop run by an older man who had a cigar clenched between his teeth. The picture wasn't exactly inviting, at least not for me, so I hadn't seen a reason to stop in once I was grown up.

I pushed the door to the shop open and the faint scent of a cigar came to me. The older man that I remembered from my childhood was leaning on the counter, a jeweler's loupe held to one eye as he examined a ring. He ignored us, even though the bell over the door had announced our arrival.

Maddie glanced at me, and I shrugged, then we headed up to the counter. We had business to attend to, and we weren't going to turn back now.

"Good morning," I said brightly. "How are you on this bright, sunny day?"

The man, Tom Robinson, glanced up at me and grimaced. He tucked the loupe and the ring beneath the counter and grabbed a rag, running it over the top. "I'm fine. What can I help you ladies with?"

"We were just out taking in the sights and decided to stop by the pawnshop and see what you had in here," Chloe said, bending over the glass counter that held an assortment of jewelry.

He narrowed his eyes. "Are you looking for anything in particular?"

I shook my head. "No, we had a day off from the ice cream shop and just wanted to get out and look around the town. We decided to stop in and see if we could find anything that we just had to buy."

His brow furrowed. "The ice cream shop? Which one?"

"Cookie's Creamery," Chloe supplied. "My mother owns the shop."

Mr. Robinson's features softened, and he nodded. "Cookie is a good woman. I've known her for years. I keep thinking I need to stop in and get some ice cream, but it seems like I never get around to it." He shoved his hands into the pockets of his brown polyester pants.

Chloe smiled. "I'll tell her that you said hello."

He nodded. "You do that. Now, what can I help you with? We've got a lot of jewelry in stock."

I glanced into the display case. There was a large assortment of jewelry. Some of it was cheap costume jewelry, and others, while looking expensive, I wasn't able to tell if it was or not. "That's a pretty bracelet," I said, pointing to a Black Hills gold bracelet that was made of interlinking cats.

He nodded and took the bracelet out, holding it out to me. "Genuine Black Hills gold. One hundred dollars."

I nodded and took the bracelet from him. One hundred dollars was far too expensive for a used bracelet, but I didn't say so. I looked up at him. "Did you hear about the terrible murder the other day?"

He nodded, his jaw clenched. "Yeah, that was old man Franks. He came in here all the time trying to do business with me." He shook his head derisively. "He always tried to rip me off. Wouldn't surprise me if he did the same to someone else, and they killed him."

"Really?" Chloe asked. "I wouldn't have thought such a thing of Mr. Franks. He always seemed so sweet."

He snorted and nodded again. "I'm sure he seemed like a nice guy. But all you two were doing was selling him ice cream, and there was no way for him to rip you off. He was trying to sell me junk. He'd be out there searching the beach for whatever junk he could come across, and then he'd bring it in here and act like it was worth a million bucks. He was crazy." He shook his head.

"I know he really enjoyed looking for things out on the beach," I said, handing back the bracelet. "That's cute. I don't think I need a bracelet though."

He nodded and returned the bracelet. "Yeah, he was something else. I had to keep an eye on things whenever he came in. I swear, he managed to rip me off a couple of times. Took some cufflinks, a watch, and a ring. Those are just the things that I know of. Wouldn't surprise me if it was a lot more. The last time he was in here I told him not to come back."

I was shocked to hear this, and I didn't believe him. "Are you sure about that? I can't see Mr. Franks doing something like that. Don't you have cameras in your shop to know for sure?" I had already spotted the one behind him that was pointed at the display case.

He nodded. "Sure, I'm sure. One minute, those things were there, and when he was gone, they were gone."

Chloe and looked at each other. "But what about cameras?" Chloe asked. "Did you check them to see if he really did take them?"

He rolled his eyes. "Yeah, sure, but my cameras were made in the '80s and they aren't very clear. I guess I need to get some new ones, but I haven't gotten around to doing it. It's not like I make a lot of money selling other people's stuff, and those cameras were expensive. I paid two thousand dollars for them brand new."

I was shocked. But that was the '80s, wasn't it? Security cameras hadn't come of age yet, and it didn't surprise me that they were much more expensive back then. "You can get cameras now for a couple hundred dollars."

His eyes widened. "Yeah?"

I nodded. "Sure. There are all kinds of setups. With the kind of items that you sell here, I think you should look into them."

He considered this. "Maybe I'll have to look into them. What else can I help you girls with?"

"Did Mr. Franks ever mention that he was having trouble with anyone?" Chloe asked. "I mean, somebody murdered him, so it wasn't just a robbery gone wrong—we don't think. He had to have been having trouble with someone, right?"

He shrugged. "How would I know? I don't know anything about Leland Franks' personal life. But I'm not sorry he's gone. I don't have to worry about him stealing from me anymore."

I breathed out, frustrated that he kept accusing Mr. Franks of stealing. He was wrong. I just knew he was. "I don't think he would steal from you."

He grimaced. "A lot you know. Why are you asking about him? Who said you could stick your nose into his business?"

The bell over the door rang, and an elderly couple walked into the shop. "Well, it's been nice talking to you, Mr. Robinson."

He narrowed his eyes at me without answering, and pulled the ring and loupe out from beneath the counter while keeping an eye on the couple as they looked over the musical instruments.

Chloe and I stepped out of the shop. "That was weird," I said. Mr. Franks didn't strike me as the type to steal from anyone.

Chloe frowned. "It's odd that Mr. Robinson had so many negative things to say about Mr. Franks. I wonder if there's something he's not telling us."

I nodded. "We should keep digging. Maybe we can find out more about Mr. Franks' personal life and figure out who would want to harm him." I was definitely going to keep an eye on Tom Robinson. He was lying about Mr. Franks.

Chloe nodded. "I'm with you. Let's get to the bottom of this."

We headed back to the car.

Chapter Seven

The following morning, I woke up after having a dream. I couldn't remember the details of the dream exactly, just that it was dark and scary, and someone was chasing me. As I lay there in bed, my heart pounding, Oliver, my cat, snuggled up to my side and immediately went back to sleep. I lay there trying to recall the dream but couldn't. And that was when I remembered something. I had passed a woman who was coming out of that narrow pathway around the rock the morning I found Mr. Franks. She seemed to be in a hurry, and she was carrying a large bag over her shoulder, one of those beach totes that served as a purse for vacationers sometimes. Then I realized that she had come into the ice cream shop later that same day, hadn't she? At the time, I thought the woman seemed familiar, but I couldn't place her, and now I was almost certain she was the same woman.

I sat up, accidentally bumping into Oliver and waking him. I reached over and scratched his ear, then got up and got dressed. I wasn't due at the ice cream shop for several more hours, so I had time to stop by and talk to Noah. First I headed to the coffee shop to pick him up a latte. I usually tried not to bother him in the first few days of an investigation, but I needed to talk to him.

I knocked on his office door, and he called for me to come in. I managed to juggle the two cups of coffee and get the door open, and I grinned at him. "Good morning, Noah."

He smiled. "Good morning, Maddie. What brings you down to my humble office?"

I stepped inside, closing the door with my foot. "Cinnamon lattes." I held them up and then crossed the small room and set one on the desk in front of him.

He grinned. "Oh, wow. It's like you can read my mind or something. Thank you."

I nodded and leaned over and kissed him. "How are you doing? How is the investigation going? I tried not to bother you about it the past two days, but I'm dying to find out what you know."

He picked up the cup and took a long sip, and then groaned in satisfaction, sitting back in his chair. "Thank you for this. I really needed it. The coffee around here is thick enough that you can stand a spoon in it, and it's nice to get something drinkable."

I chuckled and took a sip of my latte. "The Whole Bean Coffee Shop makes a good cup of coffee." I looked at him expectantly. He was going to give me information, wasn't he?

He nodded. "They sure do." He set his cup down on his desk. "So, to answer your question, Leland Franks died of blunt force trauma to the back of the head. As I suspected, he was hit with his metal detector."

"Was it a robbery? Was anything stolen?" The more I thought things over, the more I thought the chances he had been a victim of a robbery were excellent.

He shrugged. "We have no idea if he found anything of value in that canvas bag that he carried, because if he did, the killer stole it. The only other thing in the bag besides the crusty ring and some small seashells was a large abalone shell. That was the lump that you saw."

"Oh," I said disappointedly. "I was hoping for more. I talked to Bill at the bait shop, and he said that Mr. Franks had problems with his nephew. Then I talked to Tom Robinson at the pawnshop, and he said Mr. Franks was stealing from him. But I don't believe it for a minute. Mr. Franks was not the type." I felt relatively certain about that, even though I hadn't known Mr. Franks well. I was pretty good at reading people, and Mr. Franks was not that kind of person.

"He had trouble with his nephew? Did Bill say why?"

"Only that his nephew was always trying to borrow money from him. I guess it just irritated Mr. Franks, and he didn't like it. He told Bill that his nephew was too old to not have a steady job and have his own money."

He nodded and made a note of it in the notebook lying on his desk. "I hadn't heard anything about his nephew, so I will talk to him. Name?"

I nodded. "Eddie Franks. Chloe said that he worked for her mom a few years ago, just as a part-time help in the summer, so Bill may be correct in that he wasn't holding a real full-time job."

He nodded. "Great. That's great information. I'll look for this guy and talk to him. Now, what are you doing today? Are you off work today, or do you have to go in later?"

I shook my head. "No, yesterday was my day off, so I'm working this afternoon. Chloe and I wandered around trying to find any information we could about Mr. Franks. Oh. There's something that I forgot about."

He leaned forward and took another sip of his coffee. "What's that?"

"As I was walking toward the narrow path that goes around the rock there at the beach, I passed a woman coming toward me. She was in a hurry, and she had a large bag over her shoulder. Then later in the afternoon, she came into the ice cream shop."

He gazed at me. "And?"

I shrugged. "And I think it's weird. She came from the direction of a crime scene, and she was in a hurry and had that big bag over her shoulder. Then she just shows up at the ice cream shop? Maybe she recognized me. She knew that I worked there for some reason, and she wanted to check and see how I would react to seeing her again." I hadn't even thought of this until it came out of my mouth. Maybe she *did* recognize me. Maybe she was stopping in to see if I would say something to her about seeing her, or if I would act funny around her. "I don't know why I didn't realize it was her."

He took another sip of his coffee. "Okay. What does she look like?"

"Middle-aged, short black hair just a bit longer than mine, and green eyes. Like really pretty green eyes that stand out. She was a little bit taller than me and had a stocky build. I can't believe I didn't recognize her when she came in."

"Did she say anything to you?" he asked, jotting something down in his notebook.

I thought back to the other morning. "I just said hello and commented on the weather, I think. No, she didn't say much of anything other than to return my greeting and say how pretty the beach is. I'm telling you, she looked like she was in a hurry that morning. And there's very little chance, like almost zero chance, that she could have walked past Mr. Franks and not seen him. So why didn't she say anything? Why didn't she call the police?"

He thought about this for a moment and nodded. "To be honest, I'm not sure if she could have walked past him without seeing him or not. He was lying back in that alcove. It's a possibility that she didn't see him. I'll go back over there and see if there's any way to walk along the path and not see him."

"I don't think it can be done," I said, but I didn't feel confident about it. She had seen him, hadn't she? How could she have missed him? I had never seen this woman before that day, or at least I didn't remember seeing her. If she had been in the ice cream shop, she may have seen me and known where to find me. If she had only been in there a couple of times, she might not have made an impression on me. Chloe and I needed to find this woman and figure out who she was and whether she was the killer.

Chapter Eight

"Tada!" Chloe said, holding up a tub of ice cream.

I turned to look at her and asked, "What is that?"

She grinned and put the tub of ice cream into the front freezer. "After Mom made the raspberry truffle ice cream, it got me thinking about raspberries, and I knew I had to make something. This is raspberry chocolate chip. This flavor is lighter on the chocolate, and heavier on the delectable flavor of fresh raspberries, and I think it turned out pretty well."

I smiled. "Raspberry is one of my favorite flavors, and I bet it's delicious."

After talking to Noah the day before, all I could think about was the murder. He didn't have nearly enough information about what had happened to poor Mr. Franks yet, but he would get more as the investigation progressed. Mr. Franks didn't deserve to die the way he did.

The bell over the door jingled, and I looked up. My heart started beating faster when I saw the woman with black hair stroll into the ice cream shop. I forced myself to smile and greeted her. "Good morning. How are you on this lovely day?"

I glanced at the front window. It was actually cloudy and threatening to rain.

She chuckled. "Well, it's cloudy out, but I just love the rain. Don't you?"

I nodded, and Chloe came to stand beside me to check that the toppings were filled. I gently elbowed her, and she looked at me. I smiled bigger at the customer and said, "I do love the rain, as long as we don't get too many days in a row of it. But it's wonderful, especially when the clouds begin to clear and the sun comes out."

The woman leaned on the front counter. "Me too. It's like the sky turns into a work of art when that happens."

"You're new around here, aren't you?" I asked. She seemed friendly and open, and I wanted to see if I could get any information from her. How had she not seen Mr. Franks' body when she walked right past him?

She nodded. "Yes, I moved here a couple of months ago." She glanced at the freezer with the ice creams in it. "I think I'm going to get a scoop of the chocolate raspberry truffle. It just looks delicious."

The door opened again, and Estelle walked in. She grinned and waved at me and I gave her a wave back.

I turned back to the woman. "You won't be disappointed in the raspberry truffle. Cookie worked on that recipe for days, and it's absolutely perfect. Cone or cup?"

"How about a waffle cup? Maybe you can toss some sprinkles on there and just a touch of whipped cream? Make it fancy." She chuckled and moved along the counter, looking at the other ice creams in the freezer case. "Is all the ice cream made right here on the premises?"

I nodded as I grabbed a waffle cup. "Yes, we make the ice cream fresh every morning. Oh, and don't forget that you get a free cookie with your purchase. Do you know which one you want?"

"I'd go with the cherry chocolate chunk if I were you," Estelle advised. "It's delicious."

The woman grinned at her and moved over to look into the display case with the cookies. "I think she gives astute advice. How about a cherry chocolate chunk cookie?"

"You won't be disappointed," Estelle said.

"You said you moved from Wisconsin, didn't you?" Chloe asked, glancing at me. "Aren't you going to miss it?" She began wiping down the counter, but it was already clean.

The woman looked up at her. "Wisconsin is one of those inconsequential states." She laughed. "But then they're all inconsequential compared to California, aren't they?" She laughed again.

I smiled and scooped raspberry truffle ice cream into the cup. "Wisconsin is beautiful."

She shrugged. "You're right it is, but I don't like the cold."

"My name is Maddie, and this is Chloe. Her mother, Cookie, owns the ice cream shop." I hesitated, hoping she would tell me her name.

She nodded. "Pleased to meet you, ladies. I have a feeling that this is going to be one of my very favorite places in this town. In fact, this town is probably going to be one of my favorite places that I've ever lived. It's so pretty, with all the wild lilac bushes along the highway and in nearly everybody's front yard."

Estelle nodded. "I've got two great big lilac bushes in front of my house." She leaned on the counter. "My name is Estelle Smith. I used to work for the county library. I didn't get your name."

The woman hesitated as I watched her out of the corner of my eye. What was it about this woman? She was friendly enough, but I couldn't help but wonder if she was a killer.

She smiled. "I'm Olivia Reynolds. I bet your house is beautiful with those lilac bushes. I'm staying at an apartment for now, but when I find a house to buy, the first thing I'm going to do is plant lilacs. If there aren't already some there. But then I'll probably plant more." She chuckled.

Estelle nodded. "Well, Olivia, welcome to Lilac Bay. I love lilacs. I bring in fresh cuttings almost every day and put them in a vase on my kitchen table. They brighten up the whole room."

"I love lilacs, too," I said. "But I guess you had better like lilacs if you move to this town." I smiled and went to get her a cookie.

"Well, I certainly do," Olivia said. "And I love the cooler weather here on the coast. I've lived in desert towns before, and I don't miss them a bit."

"Did you move here for business?" I asked as I poured a spoonful of pastel colored sprinkles on her ice cream.

She shook her head. "No, I was thinking about retiring early, and I always told myself that when I did, I was going to do it in a place where the weather is beautiful all the time. And I couldn't think of any place more beautiful than the California coast."

"That's exactly right," Estelle said, standing on her toes to look into the ice cream containers. "I was born and raised right here in Lilac Bay, and I wouldn't move away for anything."

"Estelle, what can I get for you?" Chloe asked.

She looked up at her. "I'd like a scoop of Rocky Road in a waffle cup with some marshmallow cream over it, please."

"Oh, that is a great choice," Olivia said. "I might have to get that next time."

I topped Olivia's ice cream with a bit of whipped cream and looked up at her. "Cherry?"

She nodded. "You had better give me a cherry. What's ice cream without a cherry?"

I smiled and pulled a maraschino cherry from the jar with my tongs and set it on top of the whipped cream. Then I scooted over to the register and rang up her order. "We are so happy to have you here in Lilac Bay. I hope that you stop in regularly. We love getting to know our customers."

She grinned and paid for her ice cream. "You can bet I will. I love your little shop. It's cute, cozy, and fun. Not to mention all these delicious flavors of ice cream and cookies. I had better start exercising if I'm going to make very many stops in here." She laughed.

I nodded. "We sure hope to see you often." There was something about Olivia that made me like her. Not that I wasn't wary about her, but I sort of hoped she wasn't the killer. I liked friendly customers.

"Thank you very much. I'll be seeing you ladies later," she said, walking toward the door.

"Goodbye," Estelle said. "Welcome to Lilac Bay!"

I turned and looked at Chloe. "That's the woman I saw right before I found Mr. Franks." I had filled Chloe in on the woman, so she knew exactly who I was talking about.

Estelle glanced back at the closed door and then looked at us. "Do you think she's the killer?"

I shrugged. "I don't know. But I'm going to find out."

She looked back at the door. "I'll keep my feelers out." She turned back to me. "Mums the word. I won't let on."

I grinned. "I know you won't."

Chapter Nine

When Chloe and I got off work that afternoon, we decided to take a drive by Mr. Franks' house. Estelle had mentioned the other day that he had a live-in caregiver, and we were hoping to be able to talk to her.

"What are you going to say to her?" Chloe said as she guided her old jalopy, Brittany, down the street. It was sending out plumes of dark smoke from the tailpipe, and she had sputtered almost to a dead stop at the signal light.

"I think Brittany needs a checkup," I said as I put my hand into the panic strap above the door.

Chloe was brave enough to take one hand off the steering wheel and wave the thought away. "Nonsense. Brittany is fine. She just goes through periods like this now and then."

I nodded. I didn't agree with her assessment, though. Brittany had been running rougher than normal for several weeks, and I hoped that she did take her in for a checkup before we got stranded out in the middle of nowhere. "I'm not sure what I'm going to say to her. I'm not even sure that I know her." The name Lucy Jacobs sounded familiar, but I couldn't put a face to the name.

Chloe pulled up in front of Mr. Franks' house and parked Brittany. A hissing sound came from the engine, and she fell silent. I turned and looked at her. "Seriously Chloe, you've got to take Brittany in. She needs a checkup. She doesn't sound good."

She turned to look at me. "Maybe you're right. I'll talk to Darren Jackson down at the garage and have him take a look at her."

I nodded. We got out of the car and walked up the long sidewalk that led to Mr. Franks' house. He had owned a cute little cottage with a large front yard, and the sidewalk split the yard into two sections. A large lilac bush sat in each section of the yard. Before we could get to the front porch, the door swung open, and an angrily frowning woman holding a very large trash bag over one shoulder and another in her hand squeezed her way through the front door. She stopped when she saw us, forcing herself to smile. "Oh, good afternoon."

I smiled, recognizing Lucy Jacobs now. She had come into the ice cream shop regularly during the summer, and we had chatted now and then.

"Hello," I said. "Your name is Lucy, right?"

She nodded, looking confused. "Yes. Can I help you with something?"

"I'm sorry, I'm Maddie, and this is Chloe. We work at the ice cream shop, Cookie's Creamery."

Recognition dawned in her eyes, and she smiled and nodded. "Of course. I knew the two of you looked familiar. What can I help you with?" She still had a large, overstuffed trash bag over her shoulder, but she set the one she held in her hand down on the porch.

"We heard about Mr. Franks' death," I said, stepping forward. "He was so sweet. He would come into the ice cream shop and talk to us and show us what he had found out on the beach, and we just felt so awful for him. We thought we would stop by and pay our condolences to the family." I knew he didn't live with family, but she didn't know that I knew.

She sighed and set the heavy trash bag onto the porch. Whatever was inside made a clanking sound. "Leland was the nicest person I've ever known. I'm his live-in caregiver. Or, I mean, I was his live-in caregiver. I still can't get over the fact that someone murdered him." She wiped a hand across her sweaty brow.

I nodded, and we walked up the porch steps. "We feel the same way. It's such a shock."

"Do you have any idea who might've killed him?" Chloe asked, not hesitating now that Lucy had proven friendly.

She frowned, then nodded. "Oh, sure. I know exactly who killed Leland Franks."

I was surprised to hear this. When she didn't continue, I asked, "Who?"

"Eddie Franks. His nephew. The greediest person I have ever met in my life." She shook her head. "Seems hard to believe that someone would try to take advantage of their own flesh and blood, but that was Eddy. Now he's gone and killed him."

I was surprised she was pointing a finger at a family member, and I wanted to know what she knew about him that made her feel this way. "Why do you say that?"

She snorted. "Because all he's thought about is Leland's money for as long as I've known him. And I've worked for Leland for more than ten years. Eddie would come around here, whining and crying, and begging Leland for money. I told him not to give it to him, but Leland was a soft touch. After he'd give Eddie money, he would swear he wouldn't do it again, but he always did."

I shook my head. "Then why would Eddie suddenly kill him? If Leland was a source of money to him, it doesn't make sense that he would kill him and cut off that money supply."

She chuckled derisively. "You wanna bet? It was actually better that Leland was dead because Eddie is going to inherit his property, his bank accounts, and his life insurance policies. Now he doesn't have to come and ask for permission to have a little of that money. It's all going to go to him, and he can spend it as he pleases."

"That's awful," Chloe said, shaking her head.

She nodded, her face turning pink. "I hate Eddie. He's the most worthless person I've ever met in my entire life. I wish Leland would have cut him off years ago, but because he didn't, he's dead."

"Do you really think he would kill him, though? His own uncle?" I asked.

She nodded. "You bet I do. A couple of times Leland tried to refuse to give him money, and that made Eddie livid. He would scream at him and say that the money was coming to him anyway, so he may as well give it to him. I told Leland. I told him over and over and over. Get rid of that kid. Cut him off and slam the door in his face whenever he comes around, but he just wouldn't do it."

"It sounds like they had a very contentious relationship," I said.

She nodded. "You better believe it. He was a monster. And he threatened me. Told me that when Leland died, he was gonna kick me out on the street. And that's exactly what he's doing. I've got thirty days to get out of this house."

"That's awful," Chloe said. "I'm sorry that's happening to you."

She sighed. "I don't know what I'm going to do. I worked for Leland for almost nothing all these years. I ran his errands and cleaned his house and did whatever he needed. Mostly it was keeping him company that he needed. He gave me free room and board, so I felt guilty about taking much money from him. He gave me a little every week, but it wasn't much, and it wasn't enough to save anything, and now I've got to figure out what I'm going to do. I'm homeless." Her voice caught on the last word, and my heart went out to her.

"I'm so sorry," I said. "Do you have family you can stay with until you get back on your feet?"

She looked at me, and tears came to her eyes. "No. I don't have any family that's close anymore. But don't worry yourself about it. I'll figure something out."

We talked to her for a few more minutes before we left. It broke my heart that she was going through such a tough situation. I also wondered if Eddie really had killed his uncle.

Chapter Ten

After we finished talking to Lucy Jacobs, we stopped by the Whole Bean Coffee Shop. It was the middle of the afternoon, so there were only a few other people in the shop when we got there. I ordered a caramel latte, and Chloe ordered an iced mocha, and we sat at a table to talk about what we had found out so far.

"Lucy sure was angry about Mr. Franks' nephew, Eddie," Chloe said, taking a sip of her iced coffee. "Oh, this is good. You should have gotten one."

I eyed her cup. There was a generous amount of whipped cream on the top, and it did look good, but I was enjoying my caramel latte. "Maybe I'll try it next time. Eddie certainly has the motive if he's set to inherit all of Mr. Franks' money and belongings. Estelle said that he didn't have any children, so this nephew might be all the family he had left."

She nodded. "It's sad if Eddie is his only living relative, and he hounded him for money while he was alive. It sounds like he didn't have any choice other than to leave everything he owned to him." She took another sip of her iced coffee. "I should've gotten an extra shot of espresso. I didn't sleep very well last night."

I pulled my phone from my pocket. "I could use an extra shot of espresso myself." It seemed like sleep had been hard to come by lately, and I didn't like it one bit.

"What are you looking for?"

I glanced up at her. "I meant to look up Olivia Reynolds, but Noah stopped by with dinner last night and I didn't get a chance. I just wonder what she's doing here in Lilac Bay."

"It does make you wonder, doesn't it? Especially since she was so close to the murder site that morning and yet she behaves as if she didn't see anything."

I nodded and began searching for her name online. What came up surprised me. "Well," I said. "It looks like Olivia Reynolds has lived in a lot of different places. I think this is her, anyway."

"Really?" she asked, peering over at my phone. "How many?"

I quickly checked the sites that gave out information about addresses and phone numbers. I didn't want to pay for any of the reports, but some of them freely gave out a bit of useful information. "It looks like about eight or nine places in the past ten years or so. I don't know how accurate the sites are since they want me to pay for a report to get more information, but from what I am seeing right now, I think she's spent her life moving from place to place. Most of it here in California, but she's also lived in Wisconsin and Nevada." I wished there was a way to get this information without having to pay for it. But even if I paid for it, would it be accurate? I didn't know.

"You need to talk to Noah about her and let him search. I bet he's got accurate information about her if she's in the system."

I glanced at her. "But what if she isn't in the system? I suppose there's a way for him to run a trace and still find accurate information, though."

I looked up as Julie Rogers, the owner of the coffee shop, approached us. "Hello, girls. Can I interest you in a scone?" She held up a small tray. "These are the last two that are left, and I hate for them to go to waste. It's on the house."

I sat up straighter. "Oh gosh, that's nice of you, Julie. I'd love a scone." Julie was middle-aged, with medium brown hair and an easy smile, and right then she was on my favorite person list.

She nodded and set the tray on the table. Two blueberry scones were on the tray. "There you go. What are you two girls up to?"

"We just got off work, and we thought we would get a coffee to help us get through the afternoon," I said. "Thanks for the scones."

She nodded. "I heard there was a murder. That poor Mr. Franks. He would stop in here and get a coffee most mornings before he hit the beach. Is Noah on the case?"

I nodded. "Yes, he's working on the case. Have you heard anything about the murder?"

She shook her head. "No, I haven't. I talked to some regulars who usually know if anything is going on in town, and nobody seems to know who did it. I find that odd. Usually, someone who knows something is talking, but no one seems to know much."

Chloe nodded. "Somebody has to know something, and I'm sure they'll slip up and say more than they should at some point."

"Julie, do you know someone named Olivia Reynolds? Short black hair, middle-aged?" I asked.

Her brow furrowed as she thought about it, and then she shook her head. "No, I don't think so. Why? Who is she?"

Darn. I shrugged and took a sip of my coffee. "Just a customer who comes into the ice cream shop occasionally. She's very friendly and is new to town. I just thought maybe she had made the rounds to your shop, is all."

Her brow furrowed again. "Are you suspicious of her? Do you think she's the murderer?"

I shook my head. "No, honestly, I don't know her well at all. She's very friendly, though, and seems nice." I felt a little guilty now for bringing up her name. I didn't want anyone spreading gossip and saying that I thought she had killed Mr. Franks.

Before she could say anything else, the bell over the door jingled, and Noah walked in. He saw Chloe and me and sauntered over. "Well, I guess this is the place to be today, isn't it?"

"Wherever there's coffee, you know it's always a good meeting place," Chloe said.

Julie grinned at him. "What can I get for you, Noah?"

"I guess I'd like a large coffee with two shots of espresso and enough cream to lighten it a bit. A lot."

"You got it."

I looked at him, one eyebrow raised as Julie went back behind the counter to make his coffee. "It sounds like you've been working a lot of hours if you need two shots of espresso."

He chuckled and nodded, sitting down at the table. "You have no idea. I need more than two shots of espresso, but I'm going to pace myself." He leaned over and kissed me.

At that moment, I spotted a social media account for Olivia, and I turned my phone to show him. "Do you know her?"

He gazed at the picture and shook his head. "No. Who is she?"

"The woman I passed the morning I found Mr. Franks' body. The woman I told you about." I lowered my voice and leaned toward him. "According to the internet, she's moved around a lot for at least the past ten years."

He pulled out his notebook and jotted down her name. "I'll see if I can find her. Do you happen to know where she lives? Or a phone number?"

I shook my head. "I haven't seen a listing for Lilac Bay for her, but there is a cell phone listing for her. I don't know if it's accurate."

He nodded and added the number beside her name. "I'll give it a try and see if it still belongs to her."

"There's someone else you should probably talk to," I said.

Chloe nodded. "Mr. Franks' caregiver."

He sat back and sighed. "His caregiver?"

"Lucy Jacobs," I added.

We filled him in on what Lucy had said about Mr. Franks' nephew, Eddie.

"So he's inheriting everything?"

Chloe nodded. "Makes you wonder, doesn't it?"

He nodded. "Sure does. I'll have to check into it. Sounds like you two have been hunting around for information." He eyed us.

I shrugged. "You know how it is. There isn't much else to do in this town, and we need to know who killed Mr. Franks."

Julie brought Noah his coffee, and we visited for a few minutes before Noah had to get back to work. As far as I was concerned, I thought Olivia Reynolds looked very suspicious. Not that I was discounting Eddie Franks yet.

Chapter Eleven

Four days later Chloe and I both had a day off from the ice cream shop. Cookie was still working, and thankfully, had hired two new employees to cover for us.

"Am I really going treasure hunting?" Chloe asked sleepily.

I nodded as I drove toward the municipal parking lot at the beach. It was just after seven o'clock in the morning, and Chloe was less than enthusiastic about getting up so early on her day off. I didn't blame her, but we had a killer to find, and sometimes sacrifices had to be made. We had, however, stopped by the coffee shop and picked up large, iced coffees, each with a double shot of espresso. It was the least I could do for her.

"Aren't you excited about what we might find?" I asked.

She shook her head and took another sip of her coffee. "No. I needed at least three more hours of sleep this morning to feel human."

I chuckled as I pulled into a parking spot. I had forgotten that my father had a metal detector in the garage, and last night as I was watching an old movie, it finally dawned on me that it might still be out there. It was, so here we were. The detector was old, so I didn't know if it would find anything for us, but I replaced the battery, and it started right up. I wanted to retrace Mr. Franks' footsteps the morning of his murder, or at least the footsteps he took that I was aware of.

We got out and walked onto the beach with the metal detector. I switched it on, and the screen came to life.

"Do you know how to operate that thing?"

I glanced at her as I put the headphones on. "Sort of." But not really. It didn't matter though because we weren't really looking for treasure, we were just trying to see if we could figure out something new to add to the case. I was hoping something would occur to me as we searched.

"Wouldn't it be cool if we found something valuable?" she said, taking a sip of her coffee. "We could make our fortunes and retire while still in our twenties."

I chuckled as I moved the metal detector a couple of inches above the surface of the sand. "Wouldn't that be awesome?" I would be thrilled if I found a couple of coins under the sand, never mind something more valuable.

There weren't many people on the beach at this hour. As soon as summer started, there would be plenty of people hanging out on the beach in the early morning, but for now, we had the beach almost entirely to ourselves. We headed toward the path that went around the big rock, and I hoped that we would find something. What, I didn't know, but it was worth taking a look.

"I hope Noah finds the killer soon," Chloe said as she brushed her blond hair out of her eyes.

I nodded. "Me too."

"When we're done with this, let's go get something for breakfast. I'm starving."

"Sounds good to me. I guess we could have gotten a muffin or scone when we picked up our coffees." The detector was remaining silent, and I wondered if it worked at all.

"That's all right. I'm in the mood for breakfast. A real breakfast."

As we got to the entrance to the path that went around the rock, I spotted Mrs. Higgins heading toward us. Mrs. Higgins was probably in her early sixties and was what my Grandma Ellen would have called "pleasingly plump." When she caught sight of us, she smiled and nodded.

"Hello, girls. What are you two doing out here this early in the morning?" She wore a floppy straw hat, a yellow flowered blouse, and white clam diggers—another word my grandmother used.

We smiled and stopped to talk to her for a moment. "The early bird catches the worm." I held up the metal detector.

She laughed. "He does indeed. I didn't know you two were detectorist enthusiasts."

"I don't know if you could call us enthusiasts," I said. "But I noticed that my dad had this old metal detector in the garage, and I thought it might be fun to bring it out here to the beach and see what we could find."

"I was just telling Maddie how exciting it would be if we found something valuable," Chloe said.

Mrs. Higgins nodded. "It would be exciting indeed. I suppose you know about Mr. Franks?"

I nodded. "Yes, it's a shame. He sure enjoyed coming out here with his metal detector to look for treasure every morning. I don't suppose you heard anything about who might have killed him?" There was no use beating around the bush. Everybody knew about Mr. Franks' death, and some probably realized that Chloe and I were hunting for clues.

"Well, I did see Mr. Franks arguing with a younger man three weeks ago. No, maybe it was four or five weeks ago. I can't keep track of time these days." She laughed. "But I frequently ran into Mr. Franks, and we would stop and talk for a few minutes—he was always so pleasant—so I was surprised when I saw them arguing. Of course, I steered clear because I didn't want to stick my nose into his business."

"What did the younger man look like?" I asked, sure that it must be his nephew. If, as Lucy Jacobs had said, they argued frequently, it had to be him.

She thought about it for a moment. "Well, he was blond and balding. He was a bit shorter than Mr. Franks and heavier. I don't know who he was, but Mr. Franks didn't go treasure hunting for at least two days after that. I was surprised. I tell you, I saw him every day on my walk, and when I didn't see him for two days, it was surprising. When I didn't see him the second day, I was a little concerned."

"Really?" I said thoughtfully, glancing at Chloe. "It sounds like it must have been a bad argument."

She nodded. "That's what I thought. I wanted to ask him about it when I saw him again, but I was so happy to see him when he did finally show up that I decided not to. As I said, I didn't want to stick my nose in his business. But I did not like the way that younger man talked to him."

"You could hear what was being said?" Chloe asked.

She hesitated and shook her head. "Not exactly. It was his body language. He was leaning forward, and his hands were clenched into fists at his side. I could tell that it was a very angry argument, and poor Mr. Franks was leaning back slightly, away from him. I tell you, whoever that man was, I would not have wanted to get into an argument with him." She shook her head and clucked. "I don't know if he had anything to do with his death, but it does make me wonder now."

I nodded. "It would make me wonder, too."

She sighed and shook her head. "Poor Mr. Franks. I do miss seeing him out here on my walks. Well, I've got an appointment in half an hour, so I had better get going. It was nice talking to you, girls."

"It was nice talking to you too," I said, and we continued onto the path.

"What do you think about that?" Chloe asked. "The description she gave sounds like Eddie Franks."

I shook my head. "Why was he so angry? Was he really that dependent on Mr. Franks for money?"

"Eddie is probably about thirty years old and should be able to support himself, but you never know what kind of trouble people are in," she said as we walked. "Maybe he really needed the money, and Mr. Franks turned him down."

We still weren't getting any beeps from the metal detector as we walked. Either it didn't work anymore or there simply wasn't anything in this area. Mr. Franks had gone over these areas so many times he probably knew which areas were picked clean.

We spent an hour wandering around the area and finally the detector came to life, but all we found was an old keyring with no keys. We got tired of looking and headed over to where Mr. Franks' body had been lying when I found him. When we got to that spot, we turned around and looked at the path. There were some small bushes in the area, but I couldn't imagine how Olivia Reynolds hadn't seen his body.

"Chloe, go over there where someone would normally walk and see if you can see anything in this direction." She did as I asked, and once there, she turned around and looked at me. "Lie down close to where you found him."

I sat on the ground and then lay down near where he had been.

"Well," she said slowly. "I can kind of see you. But honestly, you're not in clear view. If I wasn't looking in your direction, and I was just walking down this path, there's a chance I wouldn't see you."

I got to my feet, and we switched places. Chloe was right. Mr. Franks wouldn't have been completely visible, but he certainly wasn't completely hidden either. Had Olivia not seen him? Or had she known he was there because she was the killer, and she was trying to get out of that place in a hurry when she ran into me?

Chapter Twelve

The following day, Chloe and I decided to stop by and talk to Mr. Frank's nephew, Eddie Franks. He had worked for Cookie several years earlier, so Chloe wouldn't have a problem getting him to talk to her. At least we hoped that she wouldn't.

We pulled up to Eddie's house, and I was surprised at its condition. It was in a shambles. Weeds grew in the front yard. Part of the peeling and tattered white picket fence was broken down, and cardboard covered one of the front windows.

"I don't think life has been good for Eddie," I whispered as we walked up to the front porch.

Chloe shook her head. "I don't think so either. I didn't know him that well when he worked for my mother. I was still in high school. But he seemed nice."

Chloe knocked on the door and we could hear heavy footsteps approaching on the other side. When the front door swung open, Eddie looked at us quizzically, and then recognition dawned in his eyes. "Chloe! Wow, how are you?"

Chloe smiled. "I'm good, Eddie. How are you doing? We heard about your uncle, and we wanted to stop by and tell you how sorry we were."

He frowned and sighed. "Yeah, I still can't get over the fact that Uncle Leland is dead."

"I'm sorry for your loss," I said. "My name is Maddie Bradford. I work with Chloe at the ice cream shop."

He nodded, smiling. "Sure, I remember you. I went in there a few times last summer to get ice cream. Thanks for stopping by and offering your condolences. That's nice of you."

I smiled. "You're welcome. Mr. Franks was a nice man. I enjoyed it when he stopped by the shop to show us what he had found on the beach."

He chuckled. "He did love his treasure hunting."

"Can I ask you something?"

"Sure. What?"

"If you had to guess who might have killed your uncle, who would it be?" I could see Chloe looking at me from the corner of my eye, and I hoped I wasn't rushing things.

His jaw tightened. "Yeah, I know exactly who killed my uncle. It was Lucy Jacobs. His so-called caregiver." He rolled his eyes. "She can call herself that all she wants, but I know what she was. She was a leech."

"Really?" Chloe asked, sounding concerned. "What was she supposed to be doing for your uncle?"

He snorted. "I'd like to know the same. All I could see that she did was get him to pay her bills and let her live at his house for free."

"She wasn't actually working for him?" I asked.

He rolled his eyes again. "If you've ever been inside the house, you'd know that she wasn't doing any work around there. It was a mess. I don't think that woman would know what to do with a broom if her life depended on it. But she kept insisting that he needed her help." He snorted. "He didn't need her help. He was in good health. You saw him out wandering the beach every day. And he liked to get out and do stuff. He liked to call it treasure hunting, but he never found much that was worth anything. It just gave him something to do, and he couldn't have been doing that if he had health issues that made him need a caregiver."

"So you really think she could have killed him?" I asked, leaning on the doorframe. He hadn't asked us in, and it looked like he wasn't going to.

He nodded. "You bet. She was always trying to drive a wedge between me and my uncle. She talked to me like trash, and I told him that she had no right to do that and to do something about it. He would tell her not to talk to me that way, but she didn't care. She did what she wanted. I tell you what, I'm gonna laugh when she gets arrested."

"Did you tell all of this to the police?" I asked. I glanced past him into the house. The coffee table was stacked with magazines and books, and there was a pile of clothes on the floor nearby.

"I told them everything. I don't know why they haven't arrested her yet."

"But why would she kill him?" Chloe asked. "I mean, if he was supporting her and taking care of her, what did she have to gain by killing him?"

"Because she wanted him to marry her. Can you believe it? My uncle was old, and he didn't have any interest in a woman. And certainly not in her. She knew if she could marry him, she would get everything he owned when he died. I think she got tired of waiting and killed him when he wouldn't agree to marry her."

I shook my head slowly. "How awful. Poor Mr. Franks must have felt trapped in that house with her. Did you try to get him to get her out of there?"

He nodded. "I told him we could get an eviction notice and get rid of her. And that's exactly what I've done now that he's dead. I got an eviction notice served on her. But I wish I had done it while he was still alive. He might still be here if I had."

"This is all so sad," Chloe said.

"You don't know the half of it. I know that she stole some of my dead aunt's jewelry. I saw her wearing some of it when I ran into her once at the grocery store. She was wearing her diamond earrings. I told her she had no business wearing those and that she better give them back to my uncle. She lied and said they were hers. But believe me, they weren't hers. She could never have afforded nice earrings like that." He ran one hand through what was left of his blond hair. "My uncle got himself in a mess when he agreed to let her move in. I wish I had known about it before it happened."

"Why did he let her move in?" I asked. "If he didn't need someone to look after him, then why did he agree to it?"

He shrugged. "He sprained his ankle ten or twelve years ago, and he knew her from a job that he used to work when he was younger. She's about twenty years younger than he was, and I guess he always thought she was sweet. Not that he had an interest in her. But when he sprained his ankle, she found out about it, and she offered to move in and take care of him. I think the minute she heard that he needed some help, she had it all planned from there how to move in on him and take everything he owned." His face turned redder the longer he spoke. Eddie wasn't happy with Lucy, not that I could blame him if what he was saying was true.

"I'm so sorry," Chloe said.

He nodded. "Thanks, Chloe."

"We were out on the beach, and we ran into someone who used to talk to your uncle every day. She said there was one day when he was arguing with a younger man. Her description kind of sounds like you." I didn't want to sound like I was accusing him of anything, but I had to know what they were arguing about.

His mouth dropped open. "What?" His face got even redder now as he stared at me. It might have been a bad idea to bring it up. "That was probably the day when I had had enough of him not doing anything to get rid of Lucy. He kept complaining about her and I kept offering him advice that he wasn't going to take. I got tired of it and we argued. It wasn't a big deal though. I was just frustrated."

I smiled sympathetically. "It must have been so difficult dealing with that."

He breathed out. "It was awful. I couldn't help him if he wasn't going to accept my help."

"I'm sorry," I said.

"Eddie, what have you been up to lately?" Chloe asked, changing the subject.

He shrugged. "I've got a job down at the newspaper delivering papers. It's not much, but it's easy work. Is your mom hiring for the summer?"

Chloe hesitated and shook her head. "She just hired a few people. I don't know if she's planning on hiring anyone else, but I guess you could ask if you're interested."

He smiled. "I might do that. I loved working down at the ice cream shop. The customers were nice, your mom was great to work for, and I got all the ice cream I could eat. You can't ask for a better job." He chuckled, his anger having dissipated. A phone rang from inside the house. "I guess I better get that. It was nice talking to you girls."

I nodded. "I'm sorry again for your loss, Eddie."

"Thanks. Talk to you girls later."

We turned and headed for the car, and he shut the door behind us. When we got inside my car, Chloe turned to look at me. "He's always been one of those guys that seem to struggle, but it looks like things have gotten worse for him. Judging by the house, I mean."

I nodded as I started the car. "I wonder if what he's saying is true about Lucy? She was sure he had killed his uncle, and now he's saying that she did it."

She sighed. "I don't know. I don't think he's the kind of person who lies, but you never can tell."

Chloe was right about that. Especially when it came to murder. Nobody was going to volunteer anything that might make the police look closely at them and their story.

Chapter Thirteen

I wasn't sure what to make of what Eddie Franks had told us about Lucy Jacobs. I wanted to believe that Lucy was telling us the truth, and I had no reason to believe him over her at this point. Anybody could have killed Mr. Franks. And that was what had me lying awake at night.

"I love this ice cream," Chloe said as she took another bite of raspberry truffle ice cream. It was midmorning, and things had been slow, so she was taking a break.

I nodded as I got a chocolate chip cookie from the display case. The coffee I had picked up from the coffee shop on my way to work was cold, but I didn't care. I was starving, and the coffee would wash the cookie down nicely. I needed to get up earlier in the morning if I was going to get something to eat before coming to work.

"I like it too. But you know me, I like all the ice cream we make here."

She nodded and took another bite of her ice cream. When she swallowed, she said, "How are you and Noah getting along?" One eyebrow arched upward.

I grinned. "We're doing great. I couldn't be happier. I just wish that we had more time to spend together."

She nodded. "I don't blame you. I would hate to not be able to see my boyfriend whenever I wanted to."

I glanced at her. "What about you? We've got to get you a boyfriend."

She chuckled, shaking her head. "I'd like a boyfriend, but I can't seem to hold on to them for very long. I'm going to have to work on that."

I snorted. "It's their loss. They don't know what they're missing out on by letting you go."

She grinned, shaking her head.

The bell above the door jingled, and Estelle walked in. She had a cream-colored macramé bag over one arm, and she wore a light blue windbreaker. "Good morning, girls."

I smiled and wrapped the rest of my cookie in a napkin, and set it under the counter where it couldn't be seen. "Good morning, Estelle. What are you up to today?"

She nodded. "Taking a walk on the beach. I'm going to have to invest in a better straw hat because the only one I have has got a hole in it. I don't like getting too much sun. It's not good for the skin."

I nodded. "I saw some cute straw hats down at the beachwear shop down the street when I was in there a couple of weeks ago. They've got lots of cute stuff there."

Her eyes widened. "I forgot about that shop. I'm going to have to stop in there and see what they've got. Maybe I'll buy two or three hats, that way I can switch them out and match them to my outfits."

"Good morning, Estelle," Cookie sang out as she carried a tray of cookies to the display case.

"Good morning, Cookie. Those cookies smell delicious."

She smiled. "Well, you had better get some. They won't last long."

I turned to Estelle. "What can I get for you?"

She rested her elbows on the counter and leaned forward. "I have some news."

Chloe jumped up from her stool and came over to stand next to me. "What is it?" Cookie set the tray down and joined us.

"Well, you know our new friend? Olivia Reynolds? The lovely lady who recently moved to town?"

I nodded. "Yes. What about her?"

"She's Leland Franks' sister-in-law!" she hissed.

Chloe and I both gasped. "Sister-in-law? Are you sure about that?"

She nodded. "I was talking to Jeannie Riley down at the drugstore, and she had just finished waiting on her. Olivia didn't see me, but I saw her, and I asked Jeannie if she knew her. She said she did because she used to live here years ago, and she had been married to Alan Franks, Leland's brother."

Chloe and I turned to look at one another, our mouths open. "Do you think she's Eddie's mother?" I asked.

Chloe shook her head. "I have no idea. That's crazy that Eddie didn't mention his mother being in town, and Olivia certainly didn't mention that she used to live here or that she was related to anyone around here."

I nodded. "She acted like she had never been to this town before. Why would she do that?"

"Makes you wonder, doesn't it?" Estelle said.

I nodded. "She's the killer. She has to be. Otherwise, why would she try to hide that information?"

"And why didn't she realize that eventually, people were going to find out that she lived here before?" Chloe asked.

She had a point. What was Olivia thinking when she didn't mention that she used to live here in Lilac Bay? I shook my head. "She's the killer. I just know she is. Does Eddie have other family here in town?"

Chloe shook her head. "I don't know. I don't remember all that much about his personal life from when he worked here."

I looked at Cookie, and she shrugged. "He was nice, and he did a good job. That was all I was concerned with. If he mentioned having family living in town other than his uncle, I don't remember."

"It sure sounds suspicious," Chloe said. "What do we do when she comes back in here? Do we ask her? Do you say that somebody saw her and knows that she used to live here?"

"We'll have to figure out a way to ask without upsetting her." I needed to think of a way to do that.

Chapter Fourteen

It was later in the day when Eddie Franks showed up at the ice cream shop. He smiled at us as he walked up to the counter. Chloe was finishing up with her customer, and I turned to Eddie. "Hi, Eddie, it's great to see you. What can I get for you?"

He shrugged. "I wondered if Cookie might still be hiring."

As if on cue, Cookie came out from the kitchen with a tub of ice cream. When she spotted Eddie, she smiled and nodded. "Well, hello there, Eddie. How are you doing today?" She opened the freezer door, placed the tub of ice cream inside, and removed a nearly empty tub.

"Hey, Cookie," he said, grinning. "How are you doing? I was talking to Chloe and Maddie here yesterday, and I thought I'd stop in and see if you're hiring for the summer."

Chloe put both hands on her hips. "Well, Eddie, to be honest, I already hired several people. They're only working part-time, but I didn't have plans to hire anyone else."

Eddie frowned. "Oh, that's a shame. I wish I had known you were getting ready to hire. I thought it was too early for you to be hiring for summer help, or I would have stopped in sooner."

She wiped her hands on her apron. "I thought I'd get an early start on it this year. I hate not having enough coverage here at the shop when the tourists flock to town."

He nodded. "I don't blame you. But if something falls through, will you keep me in mind?"

Cookie nodded. "You bet. You're a good worker, and I would be more than happy to have you come back to work here."

He brightened. "Thanks, Cookie. I appreciate hearing that. I'd sure love to come back and work for you, so maybe something will come up." He glanced into the ice cream freezer. "Say, Maddie, why don't you get me a scoop of banana walnut and one of cherry chip?"

I nodded. "You got it. Cone or cup?"

He glanced at the stack of paper cups on the back counter and turned back to me. "How about a waffle cup? And maybe you could drizzle a little chocolate syrup and add some whipped cream and a maraschino cherry?"

I nodded and slid open the freezer door. "You got it." I glanced up at him. "I saw your mom the other day."

His eyes widened. "What? My mother is dead." He glanced at Cookie, and I felt like a heel.

I shook my head as I got a waffle cup. "Oh, I'm so sorry. I had no idea; I guess I must be confused."

Chloe came over and joined us. "Your mother passed away?"

He nodded. "Yeah. Like, fifteen years ago. Who said they were my mother?"

Cookie and I glanced at each other, and I turned back to him and shrugged. "I guess somebody thought that Olivia

Reynolds was your mom. We figured she was in town for the funeral." I cringed inwardly as I said it, but I needed to know what her relationship was with him.

His brow furrowed. "Olivia isn't my mother. She was my stepmother, but believe me, as soon as she and my dad divorced, we were no longer related. At all. She was the most horrible person that I've ever dealt with in my life."

"Oh, I'm so sorry," I said. "I had no idea."

"I'm sorry that you had a rough childhood," Cookie said sympathetically.

He nodded. "Rough is right. She hated me. She's twenty years younger than my dad, and she just hated that he already had a kid when they got married. She wanted to have one of her own, and she couldn't get pregnant, so she took it out on me. Always screaming and yelling at me and making my life miserable." He shook his head. "So she's back in town?"

I nodded. "Maybe she's just here for the funeral." I knew that wasn't true, but I didn't realize that I was going to upset him so much by mentioning her.

He snorted. "I doubt it. She couldn't stand Uncle Leland. She couldn't stand anybody in my family other than my dad. And eventually, she decided she couldn't stand him either, and she started running around on him. I was never so happy as when they got a divorce."

"I wonder what she's doing in town, then?" Cookie asked, leaning on the counter.

His brow furrowed again, and his cheeks went pink. "I bet I know what she's doing in town. Bet she killed Uncle Leland. She tried to have an affair with him while she was still married to my dad. If you can believe that. But Uncle Leland didn't have any interest in her at all, and he told her to get lost. She went nuts when that happened. If you ask me, she wanted her hands on his money."

"Was your Uncle Leland wealthy?" Chloe asked.

He nodded. "Sure, he had some money. I mean, he wasn't a Rockefeller, you understand, but he had some property, investments, and cash. It's the same way with Lucy Jacobs. She wanted his money too, but she isn't going to get it."

"But why would Olivia come back to town to kill him?" I asked. I couldn't see any reason why she would do it if she hadn't been in their lives for a while.

He shrugged. "She used to occasionally send him Christmas cards. Sometimes she would call him. He wouldn't give her any encouragement, so he wouldn't hear from her for a year or two, but then all of a sudden, she'd start up again, sending cards and letters and calling. I think she just thought she could somehow sweet-talk him into allowing her back into his life, and when she saw that it wasn't going to work, she would give up for a while, but then start up again." He sighed. "I don't know. Honestly, I don't know. Where did you see her?"

I hesitated, considering whether I should tell him or not. But then I decided that I had nothing to lose since he already knew that she was in town. "She stopped in here. She seemed very friendly and said she was moving to town."

He rolled his eyes. "Great. I'm bound to run into her at some point. Did she say where she was staying? Did she have anybody with her? What kind of car was she driving?"

I glanced at Chloe and shrugged. "I didn't see a car, and I didn't see her with anybody, either. She just said that she was staying at an apartment until she could find a house to buy."

"Which apartment? One of the regular apartment complexes?"

I shook my head. "I have no idea. She didn't say."

I scooped ice cream into the waffle cup. Eddie wasn't happy that Olivia was in town, and I wondered if this might cause trouble for her.

He shook his head. "Great. That's just great. I'm going to have to deal with her now. I can't believe she would move back here after all the trouble she caused my family when she lived here. I think she had to have killed my uncle. She wanted him, and she wanted him badly. I bet she moved back to town, decided she was going to work on him in person, and he told her to get lost. She got angry and she killed him."

I put another scoop of ice cream into the waffle cup and then poured chocolate syrup over the ice cream. It sounded like Olivia Reynolds had been nothing but trouble to the Franks. But would she really move to town to try to get Leland interested in her? After all these years, did she still have her eye on Mr. Franks' money? Those were questions I needed answered.

Chapter Fifteen

Oliver climbed up onto my lap, and I scratched his ear. He had once been a stray who wandered into my life not long ago, and I was happier than I could have imagined having him around. He looked up at me with his green eyes and meowed.

"I was thinking the same thing." I set him on the couch and went into the kitchen to make popcorn. He followed me, meowing plaintively. Oliver loved popcorn.

"Have some patience, my furry friend."

When I finished making the popcorn, we went back and took a seat on the couch. I picked out a piece of popcorn for him and set it on his paw. He sniffed it, then happily grabbed it and chomped away.

"I knew that's what you wanted."

I was watching a true crime drama on television, and it was getting late. If I didn't get to sleep soon, I was going to be exhausted tomorrow, but we were so engrossed in the show that it was hard to pry myself away from the television set. When the show was over, I stretched and yawned. It was eleven o'clock, and I had to be at work at six. The ice cream and cookies weren't going to make themselves.

I reached over and ruffled Oliver's fur, and he woke up, looking at me sleepily. "We'd better head to bed now, Oliver."

He stretched and yawned, and I got up and headed for the bedroom. I was getting better at living by myself. It had never been something I enjoyed, but with Oliver around, it made it easier.

THE SOUND OF CRASHING glass startled me awake, and I was screaming before I even sat up. Oliver jumped up from his place beside me, his hair standing on end. My heart pounded in my chest as I searched in the dark for my phone on the bedside table. When I found it, I hurried to the bedroom door, stopping to listen before opening it. What was happening? I had been sleeping so soundly that I wasn't even sure. The adrenaline coursing through my body had me wide awake now, but it was hard to hear over the pounding in my ears. I glanced back at Oliver. He was on high alert, with his fur still poofed out. The room was still dark, but enough light streamed through the partially open blinds that I could see him. I turned back to the door and carefully turned the doorknob, and on shaking knees, I inched my way out into the hallway. There was silence, but until I knew where that sound had come from, I wouldn't be able to calm down.

I made my way to the entrance to the living room, and that was when I saw it. The front window had been shattered. I stood there, straining my ears to hear above my still pounding heart. Was someone in the house? All that greeted me was silence.

Gripping my phone in my hand, I tiptoed into the other bedrooms to see if someone was in the house, but they were empty. I headed back and searched the living room and then the kitchen. I was alone.

I tiptoed carefully over the broken glass and looked out the front window, but the neighborhood was empty. There was a light on across the street at Mr. Farmer's house, and I turned on my living room light now, blinking in the bright light. Oliver had ventured to the living room entrance, having calmed down a bit, and wasn't quite as puffy as he had been. I spotted Mr. Farmer coming out of his house with his bathrobe tied around him and his shotgun in his hand. He hurried across the street, and I opened the front door.

"Maddie, are you okay? I heard a crash."

I nodded, thankful I had slept in a T-shirt and sleep shorts because I hadn't even thought about grabbing a robe. "I'm okay. My front window is broken. I don't know what happened."

He nodded and came to the doorway, then stepped inside. "I'm going to walk through the house to make sure everything's clear."

"Okay." I had already done that, but it made me feel safer to have him do it too. Oliver rubbed against my legs as we waited.

It only took Mr. Farmer a few minutes to move through the house and make sure no one was hiding in a closet or under a bed. "It's all clear."

I sighed, turning back to the window, and that was when I saw it. A metal detector. Someone had thrown a metal detector through the living room window. I gasped.

"What is it?" he asked, hurrying to my side.

"A metal detector. Someone threw one through my window."

His brow furrowed as he gazed at the detector. "Why would someone do that?"

Exactly. Why someone would do that. I was getting too close to discovering who the killer was, and they were sending me a message. And I was receiving that message loud and clear.

I shook my head though. "I'm not sure. I'm going to call Noah."

He nodded. "You do that. I don't know what this world is coming to when a person can't even sleep in peace at night. I heard that thing from clear across the street."

I dialed Noah, and he answered on the second ring. "Hello? Maddie? What's going on?"

I could hear the sleep in his voice. "Someone threw a metal detector through my living room window."

There was silence for a moment. "A metal detector?"

"Yeah. A metal detector. Mr. Farmer came across the street to check out my house to make sure nobody got inside. It looks like they just threw it and ran."

He sighed. "I'll be there in a few minutes."

"Don't worry about it, Noah. I think everything is okay." I suddenly felt bad for waking him up. No one was hiding in the house, so I should have let him sleep.

"I'll be right there."

He hung up, and I looked at Mr. Farmer. "Noah's coming by." I looked up at the clock above the mantle. It was 3:30. Now I really felt bad about waking Noah up. Maybe I should have just waited and not said anything to him yet.

Mr. Farmer nodded. "I'll stay with you until he gets here. Don't worry. If they come back, they'll be having a meeting with ol' Bessie." He patted his shotgun.

I smiled. "You don't have to do that. I'm okay." I was shaken, but now that things had settled down, I was just exhausted. All that adrenaline coursing through my body had worn me out.

He nodded. "Neighbors got to look out for one another. I'll stay."

Noah was here within minutes. He got out of his car and took a look around out front before coming inside. "A metal detector?" he said, coming over to stand in front of the window.

I nodded. "I made coffee."

"I think I'll skip the coffee and head back to my house," Mr. Farmer said.

"Thank you for coming and sitting with me," I said.

"Thanks a lot," Noah said to him.

He nodded. "Any time. You let me know if there's any trouble around here, Maddie, and I'll be right over."

It was comforting knowing that I had neighbors who were looking out for me. When the door closed behind him, I turned to Noah. "The killer did it."

He nodded. "I don't doubt it." He went to the metal detector and squatted down, taking a look at it. There didn't seem to be anything unusual about it, although it did look like an older model. He turned and looked at me. "We've got to get this window fixed for you."

I nodded. "I'll call somebody later."

He took his phone out of his pocket and began taking pictures.

I felt sick knowing that the killer knew I had been asking around about them. They may have been trying to get me to stop asking questions, but that probably wasn't going to happen. Mr. Franks was going to get justice.

Chapter Sixteen

Six a.m. couldn't come soon enough. There was no way I was going back to sleep after what I'd been through. While I was tired from being up so early, I was still happy to go to work. Mr. Farmer had offered to keep an eye on the house and wait for someone from the glass shop to come and fix the window.

I unlocked the shop door and let myself in. Cookie and Chloe were already in the back, getting started on making ice cream and cookies. I could smell the vanilla from out front. When I walked into the kitchen, they both turned to look at me.

"Maddie, what's going on?" Cookie asked. "You look as if you've seen a ghost."

I smiled, imagining what I must look like. "Oh, nothing as frightening as that. But someone did break my living room window in the middle of the night."

Chloe gasped. "What? What happened?"

I shook my head, took my jacket off, and then grabbed an apron and tied it around my waist. "Someone threw a metal detector through my living room window while I was sleeping. Thankfully, that's all they did. They didn't break in; they just threw it through the window and ran." The memory made me feel a little sick. The killer was onto me.

"Oh no," Chloe said, shaking her head. She hurried over and hugged me. "I'm so sorry. It's the killer, isn't it?"

I nodded. "It has to be." I looked at her. "No one did anything to you?"

She shook her head. "You have to have a code to get through the gate at my apartments." I nodded. I forgot about that.

"Oh dear," Cookie said. "Have you talked to Noah?"

I nodded. "Yes, he came over and made a police report." I forced myself to smile again. "It will be fine. Noah is working on the murder case and will find the killer soon. Once he has them arrested, they won't be able to bother me anymore. Now then, what are we making today?"

I went over and stood in front of the whiteboard as tears threatened to fall. I blinked them back and shook my head. I was not giving in to fear. I just was not going to do it.

"Why don't you make the oatmeal raisin cookies?" Cookie said. "We're completely out of them."

I nodded, not trusting myself to speak, and went to the pantry to get the dry ingredients out.

"Why don't you come and stay with me for a while?" Chloe asked. "Then we'll know that you'll be safe."

I shook my head. "Mr. Farmer from across the street has his shotgun. Believe me, I'm safe." I chuckled. Mr. Farmer wasn't one to allow shenanigans to go on in the neighborhood. I was thankful for that.

"I would feel better if you stayed with one of us," Cookie said. "I would hate for something to happen to you. I couldn't live with myself if I knew you could have been safe with one of us, and instead, you were at home and someone hurt you."

I filled my arms with oatmeal, flour, and other dry ingredients and turned around to look at her. "It will be all right, Cookie. I promise." I took the armload of dry goods to the kitchen counter and set them down. Oatmeal raisin cookies were one of my favorite cookies.

I'd be lying if I said that I wasn't afraid, but I wasn't going to let fear take over my life.

I GLANCED UP AS TOM Robinson walked through the front door. He smiled and nodded at me. "Maddie, how are you this morning?"

I smiled back. "I'm doing great, Tom. What can I help you with?" And what a coincidence that he showed up, a suspect in my mind, the morning after someone had tried to scare me off asking questions about the murder.

He came up to the front counter and put both hands on it, looking up at the menu board. "How about a scoop of chocolate chip in a paper cup?"

I nodded. "You got it. Would you like anything on it?"

He shook his head. "No. Just a plain scoop of chocolate chip."

I nodded again. "You got it then." I turned and got the paper cup and then went to the ice cream freezer. "What kind of cookie would you like? We've got fresh-baked oatmeal raisin cookies. They're one of my favorites." I kept my eye on him.

He nodded. "That sounds great. My grandmother used to make oatmeal raisin cookies all the time, and I could never get enough of them."

"I think you're going to like these, then. Cookie has a secret recipe that can't be beat." I scooped the ice cream into the cup and then turned and got one of the oatmeal raisin cookies, setting it in the cup alongside the scoop of ice cream. I had so many things I wanted to ask him, but I didn't want to stir things up.

"So, anything new going on with you?" Tom asked as he pulled his wallet from his back pocket.

I hesitated, and my heart started pounding in my chest. *He did it, didn't he?* I shook my head. "Nope. Not a thing. How about with you?"

He eyed me as he opened his wallet. "Really? I heard there was some excitement at your end of town. I heard somebody threw something through your window."

My stomach dropped and my mouth went dry. "Well, I guess news does get around quickly, doesn't it? Yeah, some hoodlums threw something through my front window, but the people from the glass company are fixing it this morning, and it'll be good as new." I wished that either Cookie or Chloe were out front with me, but they were working in the kitchen.

He smirked. "That thing they threw through the window wouldn't happen to be a metal detector, would it?"

My eyes widened. "How would you know that?"

He shrugged. "News gets around quickly. Just like you said. I heard it down at the coffee shop. I'm sorry someone did that to you. It had to be frightening." He didn't look a bit sorry.

I shook my head slowly. "How on earth would someone know that was what happened?" Now I was really starting to freak out. How would that get spread around so quickly?

"You know how it is in a small town. Everybody talks. I sure hope they don't come back by and cause you any more trouble." He laid a five-dollar bill on the counter.

I hesitated before picking it up. "Why would they? Do you know who did it? Who told you about it?" It was him. He was the killer. There was no way anybody would know that a metal detector had been thrown through my front window. He had to have done it, and now he was warning me to keep my nose out of the murder investigation. He was here to see what my reaction was to what he had. My heart pounded in my chest, and I felt sick again.

He shrugged. "I can't tell you how things like that get started; I just know that's what I heard down at the coffee shop. I can't remember who even brought it up, to be honest."

Maybe it was one of my neighbors who had said something. As time went on this morning, more of the neighbors woke up and gathered around. Noah called for an officer to take the report, and the flashing lights let people know something had happened. I wasn't even sure who all had stopped by before I went back to bed. We had checked the video camera, but the person, who was dressed in black, was just out of range.

I stared at him, feeling a little dizzy. After a few moments, he looked down at the money on the counter. "Can I get my change?"

I nodded, feeling stupid, and rang up his scoop of ice cream and then made change for him, handing it back to him and willing my hands not to shake. "Thanks. Have a good day."

He picked up his cup and nodded. "I intend to."

He turned and headed out, and I watched him leave. My mind was reeling. Tom Robinson was the killer.

Chapter Seventeen

As soon as Tom Robinson left the ice cream shop, I called Noah and told him what he had said. I was convinced that he had to be the killer, and he had dropped by to see what my reaction was to having a metal detector thrown through my window. Noah promised to talk to him again. The results of the first conversation he had with him was that he couldn't stand Mr. Franks because he argued bitterly over the price of the things he wanted to sell him and that Mr. Franks had helped himself to some of his merchandise. I didn't believe that, and Noah had his doubts, too. I felt like I knew all I needed to know about Tom Robinson. He was a killer.

That night, I tossed and turned, dreaming of things I couldn't remember as soon as I woke. I hated this. I hated being afraid that someone might break into my house and harm me. Or worse, kill me. I hated that every floorboard squeak and car door slamming outside woke me, causing my heart to pound with fear. Maybe I should have gone to stay with Chloe or Cookie. What was I thinking?

But I somehow made it through the night, and I was never so glad when it was time to get up and get ready for work. Work would keep me occupied physically, at least. And waiting on customers and talking to them and to Chloe and Cookie would also keep my mind occupied, at least momentarily.

When I headed out to get into my car, I froze. Scratches ran along the side, dug deeply near the driver's side door handle. Someone had keyed my car. Scratches ran all along the side on the passenger side as well, but it was worse on the driver's side. My body began to tremble, and tears welled up in my eyes. I needed to get out of this neighborhood. I needed to get away from whoever it was that was doing this. I pulled my phone from my pocket and dialed Noah.

"Good morning, Maddie," he said brightly. "It's a lovely day out, isn't it?"

"Are you up?"

"Of course I am. I'm getting ready for work. Why? What's going on?" I could hear the concern in his voice now.

"Someone keyed my car. Badly."

"I'll be right there." He hung up, and I stood there, staring at my car. I had just recently paid it off. But it wasn't so much the damage to the vehicle that worried me as it was the person who was doing it and the reason it was being done. A tear slipped from my eye; I quickly wiped it away, glancing around the neighborhood. That was when I spotted Mr. Farmer coming from his house. And then Mrs. Garner came from her house next door to his. They both hurried over.

"Is everything all right, Maddie?" Mr. Farmer asked. "Should I get my shotgun?"

I smiled. "No, everything's fine. It's going to be fine."

"You don't sound very positive," Mrs. Garner said as she came to stand beside me. "Oh no. Look what somebody did."

Mr. Farmer squinted and leaned in closer. "Well, I'll be darned. What has gotten into people these days?"

I shook my head. "I have no idea. People are hateful just because they can be." I knew it was more than that, but I didn't want to worry anybody in the neighborhood.

In the five minutes it took for Noah to arrive, I looked at my security cameras on my phone, but the perpetrator was dressed in black as before, and they were sure to stay as far away from the camera as they could. Noah parked and jumped out of his car, hurried over to me, and looked at the damage to my car, sighing. "I'm sorry, Maddie."

I nodded, wrapping my arms around myself. "I know. There's not much that can be done about it."

"What are you talking about?" Mrs. Garner asked. "You've got cameras, and we'll set up shifts, and we'll watch at night."

I glanced at her and shook my head. "You can't do that. You need your sleep."

"But you need to go to work, and you can't stay up all night worrying about this," she said, nodding at my car.

"I got up in the middle of the night to get a drink of water," Mr. Farmer said. "I glanced out the window and saw someone get into a car and drive off. I didn't think much of it, and I don't know why I didn't. Some days, I just don't think right."

I turned to him. "What kind of car was it?"

He hesitated, then shrugged. "I have no idea. I'm so sorry. It was dark-colored and a sedan, but that's all I can remember."

"Was it a man or a woman who was driving?" Noah asked.

"I believe it was a woman. I can't swear to that, though. They were dressed all in black, and as I said, I just caught a glimpse of them as they got into the car and drove away. I don't know why I didn't think to come over here and check on things."

Noah nodded. "Maddie, I think you should come and stay with me."

I looked up at him and blushed, wishing he hadn't said that in front of them. I wasn't keeping our relationship a secret, but I didn't feel like we had progressed enough for me to move in with him. Even temporarily. "I can stay with Cookie or Chloe. They asked me to do that yesterday, and I should've done it. If I had, this wouldn't have happened."

"No, but something worse might've happened. They might have broken into your house, stolen everything of any value, and then who knows? They could set it on fire, or they could just destroy the inside." Mrs. Garner shook her head and made a clucking sound. "People are so destructive these days. They have no respect for other people's property."

Noah looked at me. "Why don't you go in and grab a change of clothes, and I'll wait here for you. You can stay with Cookie or Chloe for a while."

I glanced back at the house. I needed to get to work, and it wasn't like I could bring Oliver with me. I turned back to him. "I'll get my things after work. I'll have to take Oliver with me. There's no way I'm going to leave him behind in case somebody does come back."

"Maddie, did you make somebody angry?" Mr. Farmer asked, looking at me.

I turned back to him and shrugged. "Apparently, I must have. I don't know right now. But I sure wish they would find something else to do with themselves."

I knew exactly who I had made angry. Or rather, I sort of knew who it was. It was the killer; I just didn't happen to know their name. I thought it was Tom Robinson, but Mr. Farmer thought it had been a woman he had seen leaving my house in the middle of the night. Tom could have hired someone to do it, but now I wondered. I wasn't going to hang around and wait to see what else this person might do. Oliver and I were going to leave for a few days and stay with Chloe.

Noah pulled his phone from his pocket and began taking pictures. "I'll fill out the police report, and I'll bring it to you to sign this evening."

I nodded. "Okay."

I didn't know for sure who was doing all of this, but I was going to figure it out. I didn't want to live my life in fear.

Chapter Eighteen

From all that we had learned about the murder, I had plenty to think about. Unfortunately, my brain decided that it was going to do most of its thinking when I should've been sleeping. After another restless night of tossing and turning, this time at Chloe's apartment, I decided to get up early and go for a walk again. It hadn't been the greatest idea the last time I'd done it since I had discovered Mr. Franks' body, but I was willing to give it another shot. I just couldn't stand lying in bed one more minute.

The wind was blowing, and it might've been too chilly to go for a walk, but I did it anyway. I brought my dad's metal detector as protection and was casually running it across the sand, keeping an eye on the few people walking along the shoreline. I was disappointed that we hadn't found anything more than a rusty keyring the last time we used the metal detector. It would be fun if I could find something interesting; some jewelry or some old coins. My dad would be thrilled to hear I had found something fun with his old metal detector.

I wandered along the path that went around the rock and ended up near the alcove where I found Mr. Franks. I looked up just in time to see Olivia Reynolds headed toward me. I straightened up and turned the metal detector off. What was she doing out this early again? I glanced at the alcove, but from where I stood, it appeared to be empty. Thank goodness. I'd hate to find a second body back there, and as doubts about Tom Robinson's guilt had set in, she sprung to the forefront of my mind. She had to be the killer, didn't she? There were too many blanks in her story, not to mention outright lies.

I looked down at the metal detector in my hand. If one of these was strong enough to murder with, I could use it to defend myself if she had plans to do something awful to me. I wasn't unaware of how closed off we were from the road and from anybody else who might be on the beach now that I had moved to the far side of the rock. And there weren't many people on the beach this morning, anyway.

Olivia smiled when she saw me and gave me a little wave. "Good morning, Maddie. Fancy meeting you here this morning. I guess you had the same idea that I did."

I looked her up and down. She was wearing flip-flops, a pair of shorts, and a light windbreaker. Flip-flops would be hard to run in. "Idea? What are you talking about?"

Her brow furrowed. "Well, the idea to get some exercise in. I love coming to the beach to walk. It makes my calves feel like they're on fire, but I figure that's because it's strengthening them." She chuckled.

I nodded, tightening my grip on the metal detector. "Yeah, it does do that, doesn't it? So how are you enjoying Lilac Bay, Olivia? It's a lovely town, isn't it?"

She smiled. "It sure is. I can't believe how beautiful this place is."

"Oh? You're surprised by how beautiful it is?" There was nothing to be surprised about since she had lived here once before.

She nodded, looking a little confused. "Yes, I'm surprised by how beautiful it is. Are you all right, Maddie? You seem a little off today."

I forced myself to smile. "I'm great. Didn't get much sleep last night, so I decided to come out for a walk. Olivia, can you tell me why you're hiding your past in Lilac Bay? You keep acting like you've never been here before, and you're not used to the area. But that isn't true, is it?"

Her brow furrowed again. "Oh. I guess you ran into my stepson? Eddie?"

I nodded. "Yes, and he says that you used to live here years ago, and yet you keep acting like you've never been here before. Why would you do that? And why would you come back to Lilac Bay if you didn't have any family? I mean, real family, not the family you divorced."

She nodded, her mouth making a straight line. "I decided to come back to get a fresh start. Of course, I knew that Eddie and his uncle were here in town, but I thought as long as I kept my distance, I would be fine. I've always loved this town, and I felt better about not telling anyone that I had lived here before. Sure, I've run into people I used to know, but you'd be surprised by how few that has been. I wanted to leave the past in the past. And really, I don't think that I need to tell anybody about my past or the fact that I lived here before. What difference does it make?"

I shrugged. "I suppose it doesn't make any difference except for the fact that one of your former in-laws was murdered. And I happened to pass you right before I found his body."

Her eyes widened. "What? What are you talking about? You think that I killed Leland?"

I shrugged again. "Well, it sure looks like you did. Why were you in such a hurry that morning? Why did you come from the direction of where he lay dead? If you didn't have ulterior motives, you wouldn't have lied about having lived here in Lilac Bay before." These were just a few of the questions I had for her.

She rolled her eyes. "I was in a hurry because I was trying to get my exercise in. I try to speed up my walking pace to get a better calorie burn. And I had no idea that Leland was lying dead in that alcove—and I know that because your boyfriend told me when he talked to me—and like I said, it's not your business that I lived here before. I can't believe that you honestly think that I had something to do with his death. Is that what Noah thinks? Are you filling his head with these lies?" Her cheeks had gone pink, whether from the wind or anger, I couldn't tell.

"He doesn't need me to fill his head with anything. He's a great detective, and he'll figure out the truth. You may as well tell him the truth and make it easier on yourself."

She nodded. "I didn't kill Leland. And that detective boyfriend of yours had better figure that out. The person he needs to be looking at is Lucy Jacob. She killed Leland."

"Lucy Jacobs? Why do you think she killed him?"

She sighed. "She forced her way into his house when he sprained his ankle under the guise of being his nurse, and then wouldn't leave when he wanted her to go. He told me that years ago, and he didn't know what to do about her. I told him that he needed to evict her, but he was afraid to do that because she might retaliate against him. She had access to all of his private papers, and money began disappearing from his bank accounts, but he couldn't figure out where it went."

What? "Why didn't he get the police involved?"

She shook her head. "He said he didn't want to get them involved unless he knew for sure that she had committed a crime, and he couldn't figure out if she had committed a crime. Leland like to spend money. I told him to talk to Eddie, and to have him look over his bank statements. He said he would, but I didn't talk to him for several years. I didn't realize she was living with him and probably still taking money from him."

I gazed at her. "Did you talk to Noah about these things?"

She shrugged. "He only talked to me twice, and he said he would get back to me. I told him to take a close look at her, and he said that he would. I left it at that."

I nodded. "I'm sure he's talked to her." I wasn't sure if I believed her about Lucy. She'd always seemed like such a nice person, and I couldn't imagine her killing anyone. "Why did you talk to Leland a few years ago if you weren't a part of the family anymore?"

She shrugged. "Leland was the only decent person in that family. I mean, other than my ex-husband until he began cheating on me. Leland was the only person I talked to after the divorce, but we weren't close, so it didn't happen often. I would call and check on him once in a while and see what was going on. See if he was doing well. But I assure you, I did not kill him. I don't have a reason to kill him."

"What about Eddie?" I asked. "Did Eddie have a reason to kill him? He was supposed to inherit everything, wasn't he?"

She nodded. "He was. As much as I can't stand Eddie, I don't think he's got the brains to kill anyone. Oh, and I almost forgot. I don't know if this is true or not, but Leland said that Lucy had forged some documents and somehow got her name on a life insurance policy of his. I told him that's a crime, and he needed to go to the police, but he apparently never did because she isn't in jail."

"Wait a minute. She's going to inherit some money from Mr. Franks?"

"Leland wasn't giving it to her willingly, but that's what he told me. At first, he was going to give her a small amount of money for taking care of the place while she lived there, but as time went on and he became more upset with her and the fact that she wouldn't move out of the house, he said he changed his mind. Not to mention the money she was taking from his bank accounts. But then he found some documents she had forged."

I was reeling with this information. Why hadn't someone, Eddie, followed up on all of this? If he had bothered to help his uncle to evict her, he might still be alive.

Chapter Nineteen

I left Olivia on the beach and headed back to my car. I was reeling from what she had said. Lucy told us that she was being forced out of the house and had no place to go and no money. She was lying. She'd been stealing from Mr. Franks all these years. I wondered if his memory had been going and with it, his mind, and that was why he allowed it to go on for as long as it had. It was still early, but I drove by Mr. Franks' house anyway. I wasn't surprised to see that Lucy's car was still parked in the driveway. I parked behind her car and went up to the door, and knocked. I glanced at my phone. It was 7:47. No one came to the door, so I knocked louder. Then I dialed Noah to tell him what I'd found out. A few moments later, the door opened a crack.

"Good morning, Lucy." I held the phone down by my side but didn't hang up.

She opened the door wider and blinked. A fuzzy pink bathrobe was wrapped around her. "Oh. Good morning, Maddie. What brings you to my door this early?"

"I was in the neighborhood, and I thought I'd stop by to see how you were doing. I thought you were moving out?"

She nodded hesitantly. "Yes, of course, I am. I've been living here so long, that I've got an awful lot of things to move, and it's taking me longer than expected."

"So, did you find an apartment?"

She nodded. "Yes, I found a nice apartment at The Sands Apartments."

"The Sands? The ones with the lovely beach view? Those apartments are awfully expensive. How are you going to be able to pay for that?" These questions might have been nosy under normal circumstances, but she was a killer, and she had been stealing from Mr. Franks. I was angry, and I wasn't going for niceties.

She hesitated. "Yes, it is expensive. They're nice apartments, but I'll have to figure something out. I got a job in the kitchen at one of the elementary schools though, so that will help."

"I think the term for them would be luxury apartments. Right off the beach. I can't imagine what you must be paying each month. Three thousand dollars? Four? More?" No lunch lady was going to be able to afford those apartments on her own.

She frowned and put her hands on her hips. "It's none of your business how much I'm paying per month. Why do you want to know? Why did you come by?" She looked past me to look at my car, and she smirked, then looked at me. "What's going on Maddie?"

I shook my head. "I just can't imagine how a woman who was, by her own admission, paid hardly anything over the last ten years can suddenly afford a luxury apartment."

She sighed. "Look Maddie, I still got more packing to do. I've got to get dressed, and I need a cup of coffee. I don't know why you stopped by, but thanks for checking on me." She made an effort to close the door, but I stepped forward, putting my foot in the doorway. "You killed Mr. Franks, didn't you? And you stole money from him. That's how you can afford that apartment. Tell me the truth."

Her mouth dropped open. "Maddie, I don't know what you're talking about. Why on earth would I do something like that? I'm not a killer. I'm certainly not a thief. I don't know what's gotten into you."

I nodded. "You know exactly what's gotten into me. You're a thief, and you stole money from Mr. Franks, and then you killed him. You're trying to make people feel sorry for you because he didn't pay you very much money, but you paid yourself out of his money all these years. You knew that he either wouldn't notice the money was missing or wouldn't do anything about it. Or a combination of both. How can you live with yourself?" My blood was beginning to boil, and I hoped Noah could hear this conversation.

She laughed. "Maddie, you're out of your mind. You're letting your imagination get away with you. Why don't you go on home? I've got work to do around here."

"Fine. You do whatever work you want, but you're not going to get away with this."

She reached for something behind the open door, and I jumped back. She produced a wooden baseball bat and lunged through the door at me with it, and I shoved the door into her. She hit the edge of it and bounced backward while I turned and sprinted for my car. "Noah, Lucy is the killer. She just tried to hit me with a baseball bat," I said into the phone. I didn't stop to listen to see if there would be a response.

I got in my car as Lucy came at me, swinging the baseball bat. I just got the door shut when she hit my door with the bat. I tried to get the keys in the ignition, but they slipped between my fingers and fell to the floor. That was when she swung again and hit the driver-side door window, shattering it. I ducked to avoid the glass and retrieved the keys, managing to get them into the ignition this time. I started the car and hit the gas before she could wind up again, but she managed to hit the back door window as I drove off.

Chapter Twenty

Noah sighed as he took in my car. "You really couldn't wait for me?"

I clasped my hands together in front of myself and sighed too. "It probably would've been a better idea, but I suppose my life would be much duller if I had."

"You didn't want to choose dull? Because most people would've chosen dull."

I nodded. "Yeah, I probably should've chosen dull. What a mess. How do I explain to the insurance company that I was fleeing from a murderer, and I need them to pay for repairs?"

He snorted. "I guess I can give you a signed police report verifying the fact that you were indeed running from a killer. But then you'd have to tell them that you went and accused the killer of murder and that was why she came after you and beat up your car."

I looked up at him. "I'm not getting insurance money if I tell them that part. Can we just say that a masked mystery person took a baseball bat to my car? And that we have no idea why?"

He sighed. "I don't know. We'll have to work something out."

I stepped closer and leaned against him, and he put his arm around me. "I can't believe that she killed Mr. Franks. He was such a sweet man."

He nodded. "There are some truly terrible people in this world."

I looked up at him again and he gazed at me. "So, she keyed my car, and she broke my window, right? Did she confess to that?"

He nodded. "She did. That metal detector was one of Mr. Franks' old ones. She thought that would be enough to scare you into keeping your nose out of her business, but she was so wrong. Of course, I would've thought that would've been enough for you to keep your nose out of the killer's business too, but I was also wrong."

"Well, sometimes you just gotta have answers to questions, you know? Why didn't she go after Chloe? She was with me when we were asking around."

"She couldn't get to Chloe as easily as she got to you. She was told by someone at the coffee shop that you were spearheading the search for the killer, so she probably thought she needed to get rid of you and Chloe would stop."

I looked at him. "Julie?"

He shook his head. "No, a friend of hers. Jessa Karnes."

I snorted. "I don't even know a Jessa Karnes. I need to be more careful about who I talk to."

He nodded. "I guess so. But seriously, can you not do things like that? Can you leave the investigation to me?"

We looked into each other's eyes, then he leaned over and gave me a quick kiss, and I smiled. "I'll work on not doing things like that, but I'm probably not going to make any promises just yet."

He sighed. "Of course not. What was I thinking?"

"So why did she do it? Why did she have to take it to the point of murder? Couldn't she have just walked away? She already stole money from him. She could have just walked away."

"Because he got tired of her. He really wanted her out, and he finally threatened her with eviction. That made her angry. She was, of course, skimming money from his accounts. She had ordered an extra bank card, and she was using it to buy things for herself or to get cash out. He didn't catch on to it for a long time, and when he would say something about money missing from his account, she would tell him that he must have forgotten about taking the money out or spending it. Mr. Franks did like to spend money, and I guess he must have believed her for a while. Eddie said he was getting a little forgetful. And I guess she couldn't see walking away from a good thing. She got free room and board and access to money that didn't belong to her."

I shook my head. "How awful. And did she really forge some insurance documents?"

He nodded. "We found two policies that had her name on it. But it also had his signature on it, and she insists that he gave her that money because of all she had done for him over the years. I don't know if he intended to do that or not, but they do look legitimate."

I crossed my arms in front of myself. "She's a liar. She tried to make us feel sorry for her, saying she had no place else to go, and then she goes and rents an apartment down at the Sands? You have to have some money to live down there."

"Well, she did have some money. It wasn't her money, but she had some."

I chuckled and squeezed him tighter. "My car looks terrible. I've got to do something about it."

"Why don't you buy a new one?"

I shook my head. "No, new cars are too expensive, and this has been a good car for me. It's just external damage anyway. I'll take it down to the garage and have Darren Jackson fix it up for me. He always does good work." I didn't have money to throw away, so buying a new car was out of the question. I just hoped the insurance company would pay for the damage.

He nodded, and we walked inside my house and were greeted by Oliver. Noah bent down and scratched his ear.

I still hated the fact that Mr. Franks was dead, but I was glad his killer had been put away.

The End

Books by Kathleen Suzette:
A Cookie's Creamery Mystery
Ice Cream, You Scream
A Cookie's Creamery Mystery, book 1
Murder with a Cherry on top
A Cookie's Creamery Mystery, book 2
Murderous 4th of July
A Cookie's Creamery Mystery, book 3

Murder at the Shore
A Cookie's Creamery Mystery, book 4
Merry Murder
A Cookie's Creamery Mystery, book 5
A Scoop of Trouble
A Cookie's Creamery Mystery, book 6
Lethal Lemon Sherbet
A Cookie's Creamery Mystery, book 7
A Lemon Creek Mystery
Murder at the Ranch
A Lemon Creek Mystery, book 1
The Art of Murder
A Lemon Creek Mystery, book 2
Body on the Boat
A Lemon Creek Mystery, book 3
A Rainey Daye Cozy Mystery Series
Clam Chowder and a Murder
A Rainey Daye Cozy Mystery, book 1
A Short Stack and a Murder
A Rainey Daye Cozy Mystery, book 2
Cherry Pie and a Murder
A Rainey Daye Cozy Mystery, book 3
Barbecue and a Murder
A Rainey Daye Cozy Mystery, book 4
Birthday Cake and a Murder
A Rainey Daye Cozy Mystery, book 5
Hot Cider and a Murder
A Rainey Daye Cozy Mystery, book 6
Roast Turkey and a Murder

A Rainey Daye Cozy Mystery, book 7
Gingerbread and a Murder
A Rainey Daye Cozy Mystery, book 8
Fish Fry and a Murder
A Rainey Daye Cozy Mystery, book 9
Cupcakes and a Murder
A Rainey Daye Cozy Mystery, book 10
Lemon Pie and a Murder
A Rainey Daye Cozy Mystery, book 11
Pasta and a Murder
A Rainey Daye Cozy Mystery, book 12
Chocolate Cake and a Murder
A Rainey Daye Cozy Mystery, book 13
Pumpkin Spice Donuts and a Murder
A Rainey Daye Cozy Mystery, book 14
Christmas Cookies and a Murder
A Rainey Daye Cozy Mystery, book 15
Lollipops and a Murder
A Rainey Daye Cozy Mystery, book 16
A Pumpkin Hollow Mystery Series
Candy Coated Murder
A Pumpkin Hollow Mystery, book 1
Murderously Sweet
A Pumpkin Hollow Mystery, book 2
Chocolate Covered Murder
A Pumpkin Hollow Mystery, book 3
Death and Sweets
A Pumpkin Hollow Mystery, book 4
Sugared Demise

Red, White, and Blue Murder
A Freshly Baked Cozy Mystery, book 9
Mummy Pie Murder
A Freshly Baked Cozy Mystery, book 10
Wedding Bell Blunders
A Freshly Baked Cozy Mystery, book 11
In a Jam
A Freshly Baked Cozy Mystery, book 12
Tarts and Terror
A Freshly Baked Cozy Mystery, book 13
Fall for Murder
A Freshly Baked Cozy Mystery, book 14
Web of Deceit
A Freshly Baked Cozy Mystery, book 15
Silenced Santa
A Freshly Baked Cozy Mystery, book 16
New Year, New Murder
A Freshly Baked Cozy Mystery, book 17
Murder Supreme
A Freshly Baked Cozy Mystery, book 18
Peach of a Murder
A Freshly Baked Cozy Mystery, book 19
Sweet Tea and Terror
A Freshly Baked Cozy Mystery, book 20
Die for Pie
A Freshly Baked Cozy Mystery, book 21
Gnome for Halloween
A Freshly Baked Cozy Mystery, book 22
Christmas Cake Caper

A Freshly Baked Cozy Mystery, book 23
Valentine Villainy
A Freshly Baked Cozy Mystery, book 24

Printed in Great Britain
by Amazon

20486203R00068